Shadow Kingdoms

Illustrated

Tales From an Alternate

Steampunk History

Book 4

2nd Edition

Timothy M Dooley

"Shadow Kingdoms" is Book 4 from the "Illustrated Tales from An Alternate Steampunk History" series. It is the third installment in "The Adventures of Captain Lionheart" series and continues from where "Pangaea" left off, on a newly discovered Earth like planet almost a thousand light years away. It is the continuation of a short story that first posted online back in 2012.

All of the books in the Alternate History series are dedicated to all who enjoy science fiction and especially to those who remember Jules Verne and are into Steampunk.

Sincerely-

Timothy M Dooley

Another pre-determined historical event surrounding this voyage has come to pass. We are now a thousand years in the past from our last place in time. My younger self won't launch the Onyx Tower for another 1,253 years. According to the history we learned of, the Onyx Tower and its crew are now back at the beginning. We will be back on Pangaea in a few hours. This time it will be to start the second rise of human civilization on this world.

Captain Lionheart, Pangaea, 627AD

PANGAEA 627

A quiet gentle breeze blew across the small desert island in the late afternoon. Dark stormy clouds lay across the ocean's southern horizon. Directly to the south, a beam of focused sunlight emanated from the shadow of Pangaea's moon, Crystor, as it passed by. Like a magnifying glass the beam caused the clouds of the southern horizon to become hot resulting in violent thunderstorms. The dry, barren, island was dominated by a single rocky hill. The island's hilltop had a long open space, covered with large tile stones that formed a long rectangle area. The rubble of stone ruins were scattered on each side. Two large stone hands holding a pyramid, dominated the rectangle's south end. The pyramid had a large stone eye carved on the side facing the north. The northern end of the rectangle area was dominated by a large stone sphere that was supported by three columns. There was a low barrier of broken stone rubble that lay across the rectangle halfway between the two.

As the moon's light beam intensified in the south, the pupil of the pyramid's eye changed from stone to a glass material and began to glow. It grew brighter and brighter until it began to focus a thin beam of light on the sphere at the north end. A moment later some of the stones in the low barrier started shifting by themselves. It was as though many of the them had become weightless and began floating. At first, the ruin fragments appeared to be arch fragments from a building. Then, they started coming together to form a ring that stood vertically on its end. The newly formed ring was directly between the pyramid and the sphere. With the sounds of pops and crackles, a tiny ball of lightning started to form in the air at the ring's center. Once the ball of lightning formed, the beam emanating from the pyramid's eye ceased. Seconds later, a disk cloud of blue, lightning filled, stormy energy grew out from the ball until it filled the ring. With a bright flash of light, a small glowing creature flew out of the storm. Almost at once, the ring's miniature storm dissipated into thin air and was gone. The ring itself slowly began to break apart with its pieces floating gently back to the ground as they were before. The light from the pyramid's eye began to fade to a red glow, then was gone.

The glowing creature began to fly around the ruins. It was small, about the size of a hummingbird. The colorful creature was like a cross between a Siamese fighting fish and a dragon fly, only its wings were more bat like. The creatures glow had the appearance of a firefly from a distance.

1. THE RUINS CAME ALIVE on the small island as the moon of Crystor passed over the southern horizon.

2

The large stone sphere at the northern end began to hover above its support columns as the creature flew up to it. As it approached, a deep humming noise began to pulse from the sphere's interior. As the creature flew in closer, the sphere came to life shining a tiny, thin beam of light that read the creatures face. The creature commanded the sphere to lower the atmospheric field surrounding the island.

A moment later, the sphere's light and humming noise faded as it quietly floated down and rested on its pillars. The field around the island began to dissipate. The effect of the atmospheric field was twofold. First, its enclosed atmosphere made the air tolerable, regardless of what the surrounding area might be like. Second, the field had rendered the area invisible to sensors. A few minutes later, the outer barrier of the island's atmospheric bubble could be seen as it got smaller and smaller. The creature flew away from the sphere. As the bubble-like field barrier passed through the creature, the feeling was like coming out of the water. The surrounding air suddenly became very hot. Before, the approximate temperature in the field was 72°F [22.2°C]. Now it was at least 120°F [45°C]. The creature communicated with the sphere again to make the atmospheric field intermittent. It knew the dark cloud of death that once encircled the planet was gone and humans that had arrived recently were watching.

2. FLYING CLOSE TO THE SPHERE, the creature communicated its intentions.

Captains Log: Our voyage elapsed time is now 169 days (Dec 10th, 1627, Earth Time)

12:00 Hours:

The exploration of underground city of Velesten is nearly complete. The name was derived from the Slavic God of Veles. It came at the suggestion of chief engineer Petrov. He told us Veles was a major god of the earth and the underworld according to the beliefs of his distant ancestors. Dr. Holsten thinks the city of Velesten could accommodate up to 100,000 people.

It's funny how every question answered only reveals at least ten more questions. After further examination, it would seem Velesten might have been much more than just an underground city. The remains of the portal that was discovered in a lower chamber suggests it was used as a means of escape for thousands, perhaps millions of people when Pangaea came under siege by the death cloud. What is even more incredible is some of the portal's remains seen to indicate that my friend and colleague Margret Dana might have visited here at some time in the distant past. I think she had the portal built in an effort to save as many people as she could by sending them to a safe place off world. For now, it is only a theory.

At first I wondered how she could possibly know about Pangaea's history. Then I remembered the book she gave to me before we departed Earth and told me I'm going to have an encounter with a younger version of her when I am much older many years from now. I recall her telling me of the possibility of portal time travel. I'm probably getting ahead of myself. As I stated, it is only a theory.

When we first arrived at Pangaea, West reported there were several small areas that had the same surface temperature in spite of their surroundings having vastly different weather conditions. I wasn't sure which one to explore first until our sensors detected an unusual anomaly several hundred miles directly south of us. It's 137 miles north of the equator, or perhaps I should say 37 miles above the hot region we christened "The Moon Belt". Based on the images West showed me, it looks to be a small island that has unnatural features that disappear, then reappear at regular intervals. Based on the scan images, the area of interest appears to be a ruin monument of some kind that is relatively intact. I am curious how it survived the death cloud that once encircled this planet. I hope it will reveal more clues to the civilization that once existed here. I had the Onyx Tower set down in the sea just off the island's north coast. We plan to..."

"Captain?" West said on the com, interrupting.

"Lionheart. Go ahead West."

"Captain, I received the latest detailed telemetry images of the island," West responded.

"I'm on my way. Lionheart out."

Lionheart wasted no time getting to the Wardroom. "Ok West, what do you have?" he asked, stepping up to the table.

"It appears to be the ruins of a temple site at the top of the island. There seems to be an intermittent effect in the shape of a dome over the site," West said.

Explain?" Lionheart asked.

"At precise eleven-minute intervals, the ruin site becomes visible then invisible with only natural ground features detected. During the time the site is visible, sensors indicate the temperature there is +122.3°F [+45°C]. When the site becomes invisible its temperature suddenly drops down to +72°F [+22.2°C]". This infrared image shows the dome shaped temperature field during the cooler interval. There is a sphere among the ruins, and it is at the center of the dome field. Its position would suggest it is the energy source of the field surrounding the site," West responded.

"Interesting. I wonder if the other temperature anomalies we detected on this planet are also artificially created by a live energy source. If so, there could be other ruin sites on this planet's surface we haven't seen yet," Lionheart said.

"If this field was able to block our sensors, it's also possible it could block the presence of any living beings," West said.

6

"What are you suggesting?"

"I'm suggesting the possibility if this field shielded the ruin site from our sensors, it might also have been shielded from the death cloud. If so, anyone living in there would have been safe and may still be around," West said.

3. CAPTAIN LIONHEART MEETS with his officers in the wardroom to review images of newly discovered ruins on a remote island near Pangaea's equator.

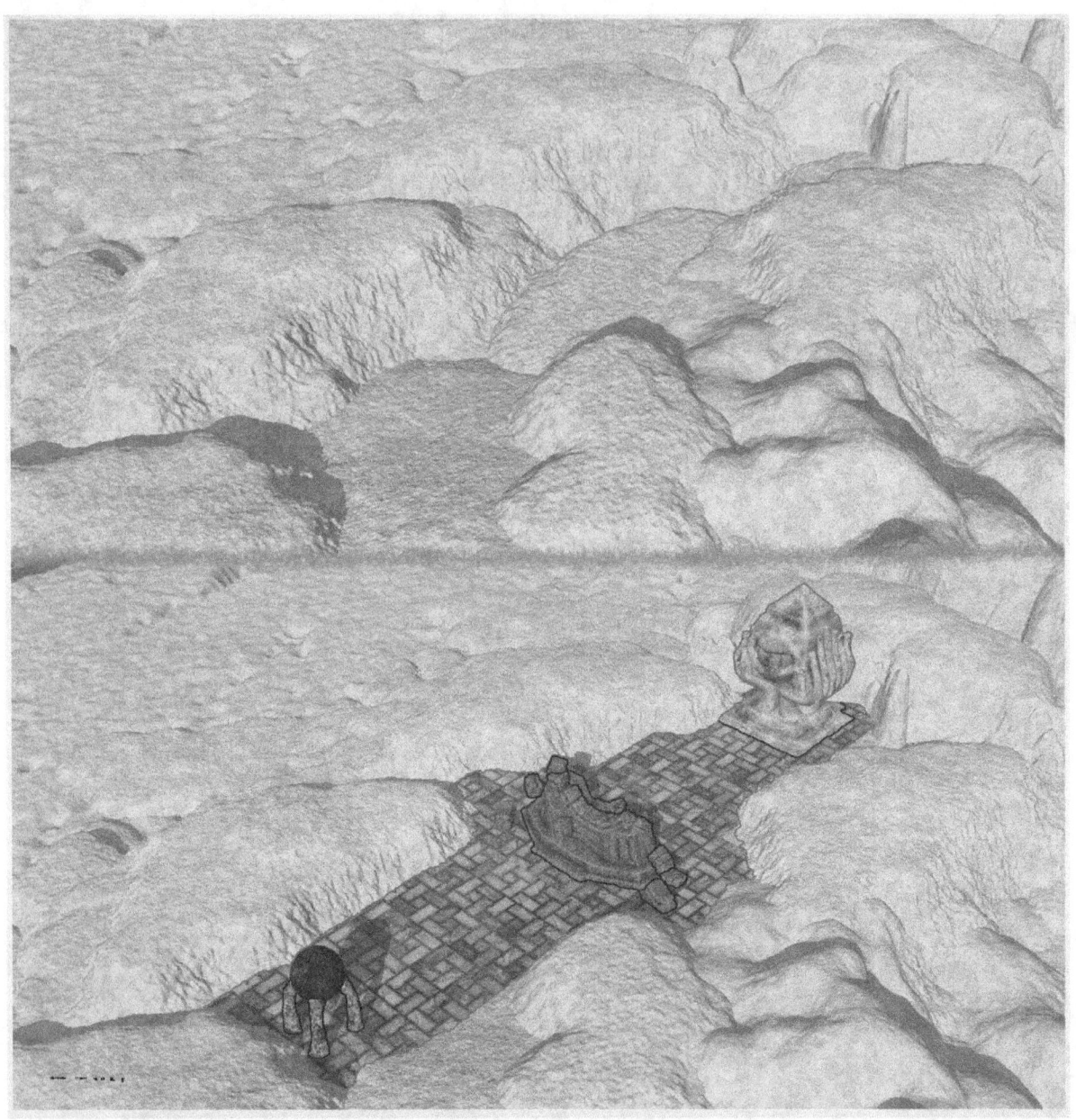

4. PRELIMINARY IMAGES OF THE remote island revealed ruins when the site temperature changed to match surrounding weather. **Above:** Only natural features were detected with the site temperature was +72°F [+22.2°C]". **Below:** Ancient ruins were detected with the site temperature was the same as the surrounding area.

"We will find out soon enough. Mr. Thornton".

"Aye Captain."

"Prepare a rotor craft for immediate launch. West, I want you, Connors, Holston and Mullin to accompany me," Lionheart commanded.

"Aye Sir," Thornton responded.

A short time later the rotorcraft lifted off from the tower and headed south to the island. As they approached, it appeared mostly barren and lifeless.

"I don't see anything," Holsten said.

"The interval for the anomaly to reappear is four minutes from now," West said as they passed over the islands coast.

There was a sudden jolt to the rotorcraft. At the same time, the site of ruins appeared below. Light desert foliage also appeared. Lionheart looked over at West. He was expecting her to say something, but she sat quietly. West always had a somewhat blank expression on her face when she was receiving telemetry.

"West? What is it?" Lionheart asked.

"Curious. The next interval for the anomaly to appear was three minutes, 43 seconds from now. I have also detected a sudden drop in temperature. The outside temperature is now +72°F [+22.2°C]. It would seem that we just passed through an atmospheric barrier of some kind. I've also lost contact with the tower," West said.

At that very moment at the Onyx Tower, the signal from Lionheart's rotorcraft was lost. "Mr. Thornton, Sir, the Captain's rotorcraft has vanished from our sensors. It's gone, Sir," Officer Stone said.

"You mean we only lost his signal; the rotorcraft is still there, right?" Thornton asked, as his came over to look at Stone's control panel.

"No Sir. The rotorcraft is gone. One moment it was there, the next it isn't. I'm going to run a diagnostic on our sensor systems now. We will have the results in a minute or two," Stone said.

5. LIONHEART AND HIS PARTY lift off from the tower in their rotorcraft.

"Very well. Mr. Petrov," Thornton asked.

"Petrov here."

"Mr. Petrov, I want a second rotorcraft readied as soon as possible. Peterson will pilot, Dorian and Moss will go with him. Standby and await my orders."

"Aye Sir," Petrov responded.

Lionheart's rotorcraft approached the area of interest. After circling the ruins, they landed in a flat open area nearby. Once on the ground, the party got out and walked toward the ruins.

"Holston, what do you make of this?" Lionheart asked.

"It appears to be the remains of a possible place of worship. I'm curious about the human eye on the pyramid. It reminds me of a Masonic symbol back on Earth," Holston said.

"It makes me think of the 'all seeing eye' or 'the eye of providence' found on the American dollar. To some the pyramid represents the home and the eye represents the homeowner. Whatever blocked this place from our sensors must also have blocked detection from the death cloud. I have a feeling we disappeared from ships sensors when we passed through that atmospheric barrier. It's my guess Thornton will send a second rotor craft to investigate. I think this barrier field was used to hide this site from the death cloud," Lionheart said.

They looked closer. The hands holding the pyramid up looked human in every respect except each hand had eight fingers. The pupil of the pyramid's eye was made of a green crystalline material. To Dr. Holsten, it looked like a rare stone one would expect to see in the statue of an ancient deity. As he continued to study it, Lionheart and West examined the area. West noticed the pyramid's eye looked directly across the area toward the sphere.

6. **AS THE LANDING PARTY EXPLORED** the site of the alien ruins, Lionheart could not escape the feeling the site was somehow related to the dreams he had been having lately.

"Captain, the glass pupil of the pyramid's eye appears to be the tip of a prism that focuses a beam of intense energy directly at the sphere. Judging by the pyramid's position, I would suggest the beam becomes active every time the moon passes across the equator south of us," West said.

"To what end?" Lionheart asked.

"A preliminary scan indicates both the sphere, and the pyramid seem to be approximately the same age. The sphere has a strong energy reading and is undoubtedly the source of the field disturbance over the island. I think the pyramid's beam may be a way of recharging the sphere, but I won't know until I have had a chance to observe it more closely. According to the intervals we have observed, the field emanating from it should collapse approximately thirty seconds from now," West said.

"Holston, how old do you think this site is?" Lionheart asked.

"I can't say for sure. Based on these readings, my guess would be at least three thousand years. I'll know more when I get samples back to the ship for carbon dating," Holsten said.

"All right, we'll return to the tower after you have collected some samples," Lionheart said.

"Captain look," West said.

There was a disturbance in the air all around them. It looked like they were in a dome that covered the island, and it was getting smaller and smaller. It reminded Lionheart of the surface of water as seen from underneath. As the dome wall got closer, the air distortion became more visible. A moment later, it passed through them. The air suddenly became much hotter. At the same moment, contact with the tower was restored and West detected a second Rotorcraft was closing on their position.

7. AS THEY WATCHED, the atmospheric energy field collapsed into the sphere. Just before collapsing, it had the appearance of a ball of rough water encapsulating the sphere.

"Yes. Interesting," West quietly said to herself. "Captain, the field over this area has terminated."

"Look," Mullin said as he motioned at the sphere.

As they watched, the atmospheric energy field collapsed into the sphere. Just before collapsing, it had the appearance of a ball of rough water encapsulating the sphere.

"Captain, Peterson here. Do you need assistance?"

"Peterson, this is Lionheart. We are in no need of assistance and are returning to the tower. Lionheart out."

"Aye Sir." Peterson responded as his rotorcraft passed overhead and headed back. Moments later, Lionheart's party lifted off.

Knowing the site was still active, West kept her hand-held scanner on the entire time. Just as they climbed aboard the rotorcraft, it detected a slight drop in air pressure and a static electric field. It lasted only for a second or two, then reoccurred several times as they flew back to the tower.

Alone in his cabin, Lionheart looked out at the sunset. For a moment, he was reminded of Earth. It quickly went away when he looked up at Torlon, Pangaea's red sister planet and the green nebula in the sky beyond. He thought about the ruin site and the field surrounding it and wondered about the possibility that other active sites might exist on Pangaea. He also wondered if they were beyond detection of ship's sensors, could they have also escaped detection from the death cloud that once encircled the planet. Lionheart suddenly had the feeling that someone was in his cabin.

"Captain," a voice said from behind him.

Somewhat startled, Lionheart suddenly turned around. No one was there. Lionheart took a deep breath. He wondered if his imagination might be getting the best of him.

He thought for a moment. The voice he heard was familiar. He had heard it before, but from where?

Captains Log: Our voyage elapsed time is now 172 days (Dec 13th, 1627, Earth Time)

04:00 Hours:

It has been three days since our first contact with the newly discovered ruin site. Several teams have visited the site to learn as much as possible about the source of the atmospheric field that phases in and out. The nature of the field and the power source behind it clearly suggests a highly advanced science that is beyond our current understanding. West has been very diligent to record and catalog every aspect of the sphere's observable properties. I have recorded some of West's notes in the back of a journal given to me by Margret Dana, per her request.

Since returning from the site, we christened "Crystor's Gate Island", I've had the unshakeable feeling that I am not alone. It is as though there is a ghost in my quarters that comes to me in my dreams at night. Throughout my life, I have experienced several vivid dreams, well beyond what would be considered normal. But in the last few nights, I had a reoccurring dream that seems almost real. Until now, I have kept it to myself, fearing that Connors might place me under observation. However, because of their nature, I have decided to hold a meeting and reveal my dreams detail. I have already submitted sketches and marked up maps based on my dreams to our ship's head Cartographer, Jane McRandell.

Peter M Lionheart, Captain

After receiving the completed maps and star charts from McRandell, Lionheart sent for West.

"Reporting as ordered Captain," West said entering Lionheart's cabin.

"Come in West. I want to show you something," Lionheart said as he motioned to the maps spread out across his desk.

"Interesting. These are highly detailed. I see you have labeled all land areas and bodies of water. I am curious as to what inspired these names," West said looking at the maps of Pangaea.

"They came to me in a dream. I had McRandell create these maps based on several sketches and markups I did. I'll explain later. Right now, there is something I want you to do for me. When we were at the ruin site earlier, you recorded a temperature of +72°F [+22.2°C] when the atmospheric shield was active," Lionheart said.

"Yes. What do you what me to do?" West asked.

"I want to run an infrared survey of the entire planet. More specifically, I want you to look for any other places where the surface temperature is the same as this site. I am also interested in any areas that have an unusual temperature variance from their surroundings," Lionheart said.

"I take it you mean warm areas in the artic or cool areas in hot deserts or the moon belt," West said.

"Precisely," Lionheart said.

"We'll need to move the tower into space to conduct the survey," West said.

"I'll give the order as soon as we are through exploring the ruin site. In addition, there is one more thing. I am especially interested in three locations in the northern hemisphere: Amadosa, Caperniea and Invergal. Their locations are labeled on this map," Lionheart said.

"Why are you interested in these specific areas?" West asked looking closer at one of the maps.

8. ALONE WITH WEST IN HIS CABIN, Lionheart revealed maps that had most land and sea features labeled. When questioned about it, Lionheart said the names came to him over the course of several dreams.

"If my guess is correct, we are going to find a lot more than what we found at the site here," Lionheart said.

The last two rotorcrafts set down near the ruin site. The island survey was nearly complete. It wasn't long until Petrov and his engineering team were completing their examination of the ruins. The heat was oppressive. Petrov knew the atmospheric field would be phasing back on. He wanted to be on the island when it happened, so he could record another scan to monitor the changes. Among Petrov's party was mechanical engineer, Alexi Ivanov, the wounded survivor Lionheart picked up in Russia just before departing Earth. Since being on board, Ivanov showed an outstanding aptitude for science and engineering. Even though he was picked up in the earth year of 1627, Ivanov seemed centuries ahead of his time. Since being on board, Petrov seemed determined to teach him everything he could. He believed Ivanov would make a great asset to the tower's engineering team. Lionheart believed he was the genius behind the Vladislav Empire in western Siberia.

Unlike the others, Ivanov stopped exploring when he saw the eye on the pyramid face. Somehow, he knew what it was. Before leaving Earth, he remembered his guardian appearing before him, telling him he would appear again soon after seeing the "Eye of Crystor". The sphere gave off a deep pulse. It startled everyone. Shortly after the pulse began, it looked like it was encapsulated in water. The field quickly expanded outward. Everyone had a feeling of relief as the atmospheric field boundary engulfed the site. The temperature dropped back to a cool +72°F [+22.2°C]. Back at the tower, West became aware that the field was up, as contact with the landing party was lost. For a moment West felt concern, but decided not to respond, knowing Petrov's party would return safely. Petrov didn't know what to make of his scans. It re-confirmed the technology of the ancient sphere was clearly beyond his current understanding. It would take time to make sense of his readings. Having satisfied himself, Petrov decided it was time to return to the Tower. Finding faint traces of electromagnetism on some of the stone ruins, Engineer Malcom, the second in command, wanted to finish his scans. Petrov agreed, allowing the party to stay a little longer.

9. **CREWMAN IVANOV WAS STUNNED** when he realized he was looking up at the "Eye Of Crystor". It was the monument his guardian had spoken of earlier.

Ivanov helped Malcom with his equipment, but soon after found himself at the base of the pyramid, looking up at the eye. Suddenly the face of the pyramid turned blue from a flashing light that was behind him. He slowly turned around, covering his eyes with his head lowered.

"Master. I've done as you asked," Ivanov said, looking down and dropping to one knee. "For a moment, I didn't think we would survive the death cloud. I did as you asked. When we were inside the moon, I sent the transmission. What happens now?" Ivanov asked.

"You've done exactly as I asked. You have come a thousand light years from Earth, but your journey is only half-complete. You must stay with the tower and travel back into the distant past. In the north polar region of this planet there is an island group called Amadosa. They are ruled by a powerful Queen. I want you to give this to her. You will know when the time is right. She is expecting you," the guardian said as he placed a small vial in the palm of Ivanov's outstretched hand. "Beyond that, there is nothing you must do. You must become invisible, blend in with Petrov's crew and stay with the tower. Lionheart has already encountered the ghost that will lead him back in time. When you have arrived, you will see me again. Fear not for your crewmates. They will awaken once I'm gone," the guardian said.

Looking down, Ivanov could see the blue light was fading. He slowly uncovered his eyes as he looked up. He could see Malcom and Peterson passed out on the ground not far away. He helped them get back up saying another pulse from the sphere had rendered all of them unconscious. After gathering their equipment, they returned to the tower.

After receiving Petrov's party, the tower ascended into space. The drones for surveying Pangaea's surface temperature were launched shortly after reaching space. A short time later, Lionheart watched from his cabin window as they returned one by one. He knew West would process the telemetry very quickly. An hour later he met with his chief officers in the Wardroom. The maps Jane McRandell created were spread out on the conference table in front of them. West arrived with the infrared images created from the recent planetary survey.

"Captain, I have surveyed the planet as ordered. Only one atmospheric anomaly was detected in the three areas of interest," West said.

"Captain?" Thornton asked.

"I'll explain. Before calling all of you here, I wanted verification. Something is happening to me that I don't fully understand. Since returning from the ruin site three days ago, I experienced three reoccurring dreams that remain very clear to me, even after I'm awake," Lionheart said.

"Captain, on our first arrival in this part of space when we encountered the rogue planet before coming to this system, you said a voice was calling for you. Is there any relationship between it and the dreams you're having?" Connors asked.

"Yes, only the recent dreams have been more intense. In the first dream, I found myself standing on a flat, calm beach. I saw the Onyx Tower on the shoreline at the far end of it. There was a portal in the sky beyond the tower. It was outlined with blue clouds, filled with lightning. The hole was the entrance to another time storm, similar the one we encountered over Neptune. As I started to walk towards the tower, it lifted off and started to head into the portal. Just as it was about to enter something stopped it. Then, the tower itself started breaking up into the pieces. I had the feeling it was being erased from existence. As I started running towards it, I felt myself being pulled backwards through a doorway. Looking back, I saw the last part of the tower breakup into thin air. As I stepped back toward the opening, the door suddenly slammed shut. It closed so violently I was knocked down. At first, I was surrounded in darkness. When I got back up on my feet, I found myself standing in the rear garden of my Aunt Fern's house back in London. As I approached the back door, I noticed a lock with three keyholes," Lionheart said. Everyone was quiet.

"What happen then?" Connors asked, breaking the silence.

"I heard a voice from someone standing in the shadows behind me. It said, *For the tower to reach its place, you need three keys, the Amadosa, Caperniea and Invergal.* The voice was the same one I had in my dream when we first encountered the rogue planet. I also heard it in my cabin when I first arrived back from Crystor's Gate Island," Lionheart said.

"Please go on with your dream," Connors said.

"I turned to see who it was, but the garden was dark. I could only see his outline. He was like a ghost. Despite that, I had a feeling that the visitor was friendly. Call it what you will, my first impression was as though he was some sort of guardian angel who was trying to help us. That was the end of the first dream." Lionheart said.

"Curious names for keys. Do you know what they mean?" West asked.

"Interesting maps. I see you have labeled Pangaea in detail," Thornton said, looking down at the maps on the table.

"The meaning of those keys and the detail on these maps you see before you are the result of my second dream. The visitor came to me again. This dream wasn't as dramatic as the first. It mostly consisted of a conversation with the visitor who identified himself as Argosh. I never saw his face clearly, nor do I remember our exact conversation, but when I awoke, I had a clear knowledge of the named features on Pangaea, this solar system, and also the trinary star system we are in. The first thing I did was create detailed sketches and markups of everything I remembered and submitted them to McRandell to have maps made. In addition to map detail, Argosh explained a brief history of this trinary star system," Lionheart said, stopping for a moment.

"Doctor Connors, as for the names of the keys you asked about, I had no idea at first, but those names are actually three locations on Pangaea," Lionheart said.

10. EMERSED IN A POWERFUL DREAM, Lionheart found himself in the back garden of his ant Fern's house in London. As he approached the back door he noticed it had a three-lock box.

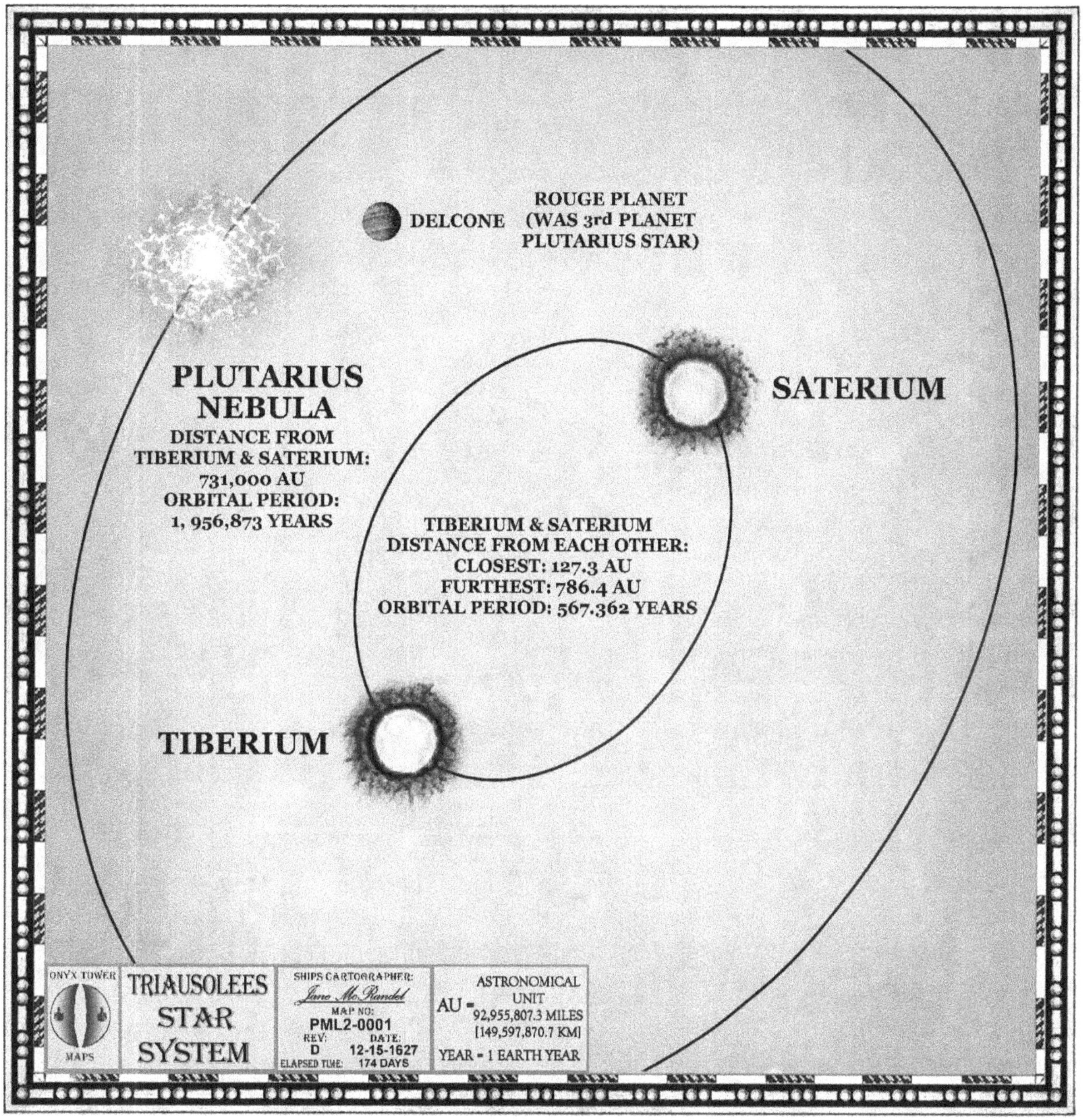
ROUGE PLANET
(WAS 3rd PLANET
PLUTARIUS STAR)
DELCONE
PLUTARIUS
NEBULA
DISTANCE FROM
TIBERIUM & SATERIUM:
731,000 AU
ORBITAL PERIOD:
1, 956,873 YEARS
SATERIUM
TIBERIUM & SATERIUM
DISTANCE FROM EACH OTHER:
CLOSEST: 127.3 AU
FURTHEST: 786.4 AU
ORBITAL PERIOD: 567.362 YEARS
TIBERIUM
ONYX TOWER
MAPS
TRIAUSOLEES
STAR
SYSTEM
SHIPS CARTOGRAPHER:
MAP NO:
PML2-0001
REV:
D
DATE:
12-15-1627
ELAPSED TIME: 174 DAYS
ASTRONOMICAL
UNIT
AU = 92,955,807.3 MILES
[149,597,870.7 KM]
YEAR = 1 EARTH YEAR

11. THE FIRST MAP LIONHEART REVEALED, an earlier version of the one shown above. It was of the Triausolees star system with names as revealed by the voice of someone who called himself Argosh.

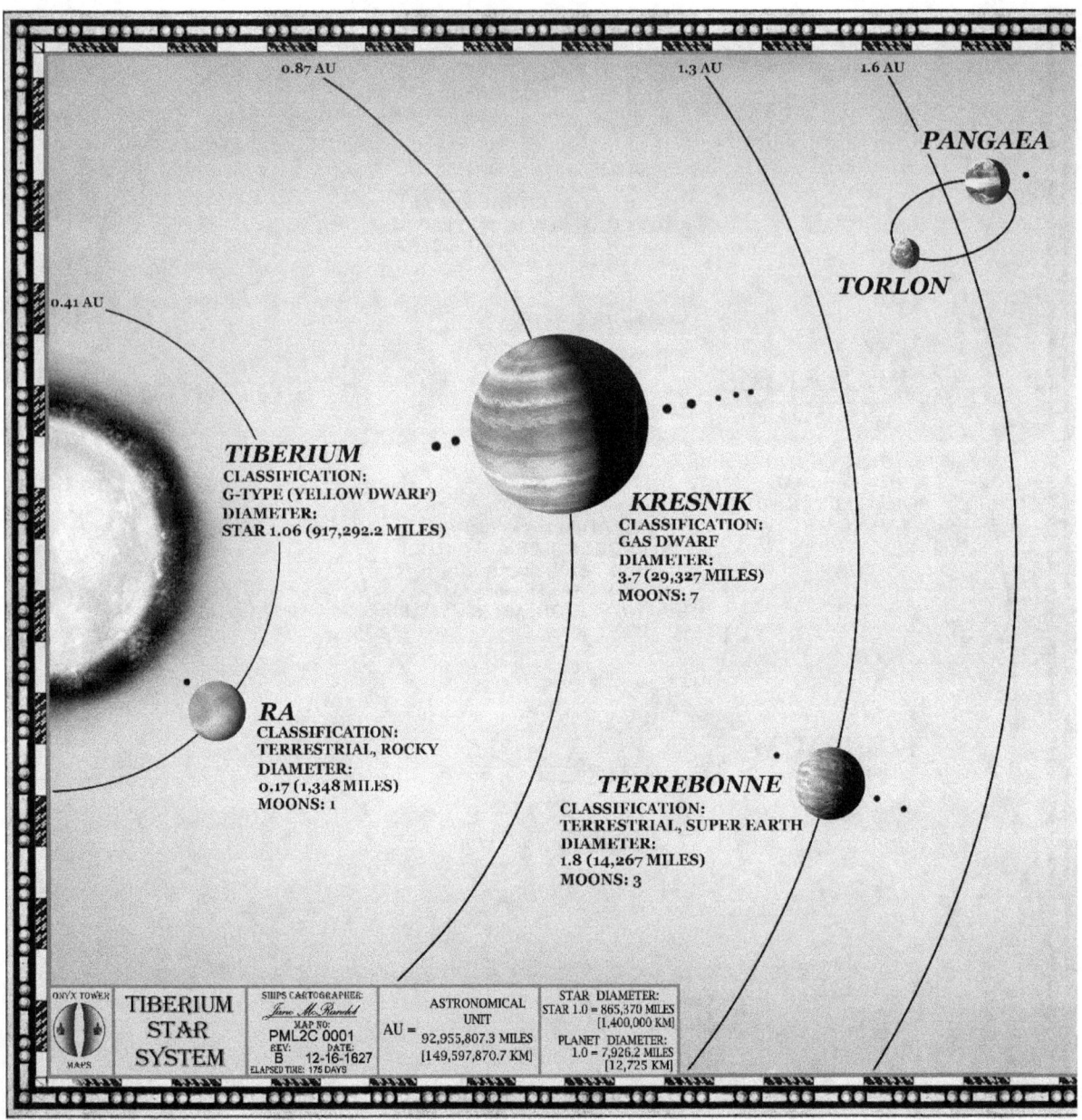

12. THE SECOND MAP LIONHEART REVEALED an earlier version of the one shown above. It was of the Tiberium star system. Argosh revealed the names of all the planets. The basic data of each planet was provided by the ship's sensors.

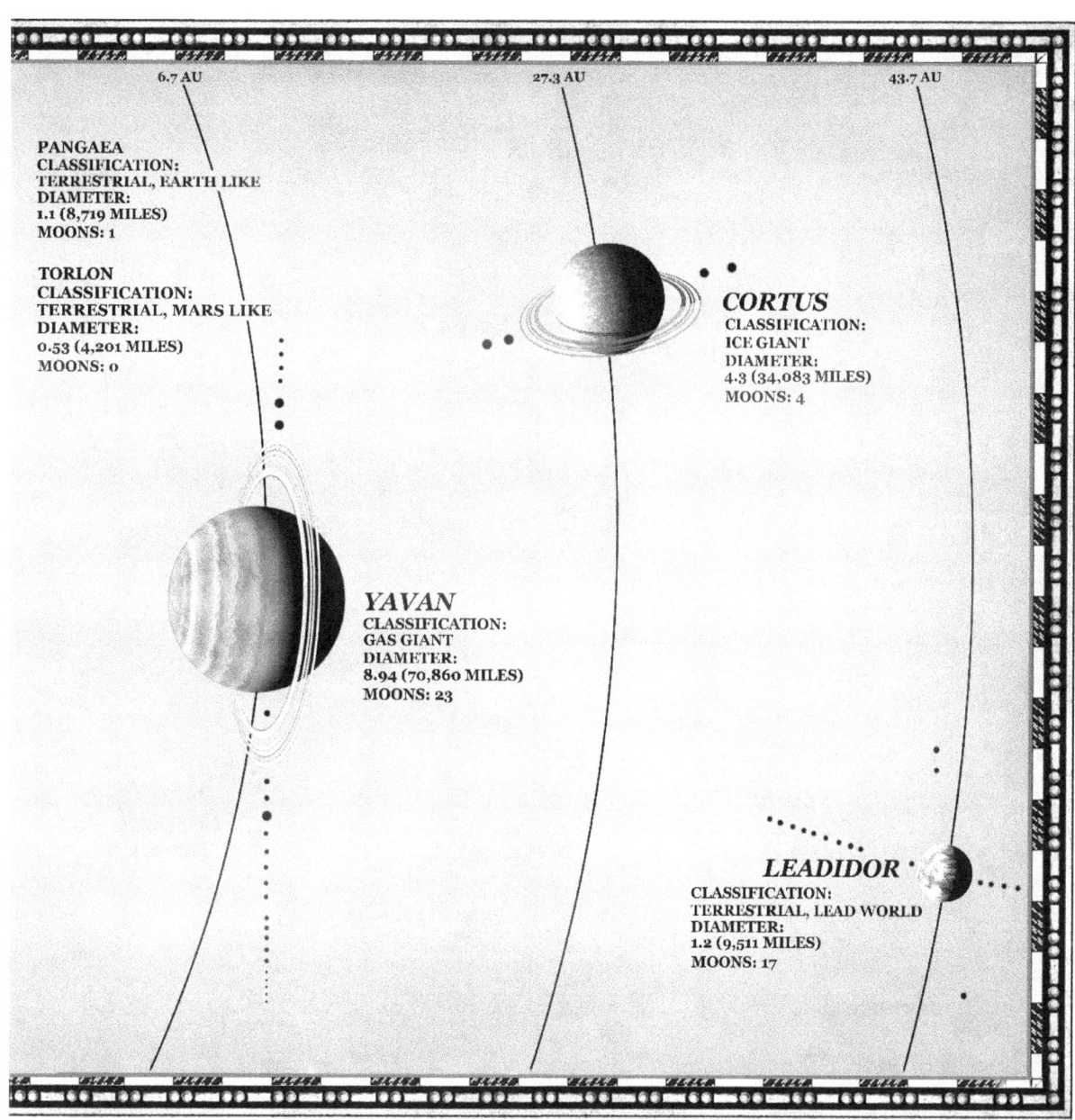

6.7 AU   27.3 AU   43.7 AU

PANGAEA
CLASSIFICATION:
TERRESTRIAL, EARTH LIKE
DIAMETER:
1.1 (8,719 MILES)
MOONS: 1

TORLON
CLASSIFICATION:
TERRESTRIAL, MARS LIKE
DIAMETER:
0.53 (4,201 MILES)
MOONS: 0

CORTUS
CLASSIFICATION:
ICE GIANT
DIAMETER:
4.3 (34,083 MILES)
MOONS: 4

YAVAN
CLASSIFICATION:
GAS GIANT
DIAMETER:
8.94 (70,860 MILES)
MOONS: 23

LEADIDOR
CLASSIFICATION:
TERRESTRIAL, LEAD WORLD
DIAMETER:
1.2 (9,511 MILES)
MOONS: 17

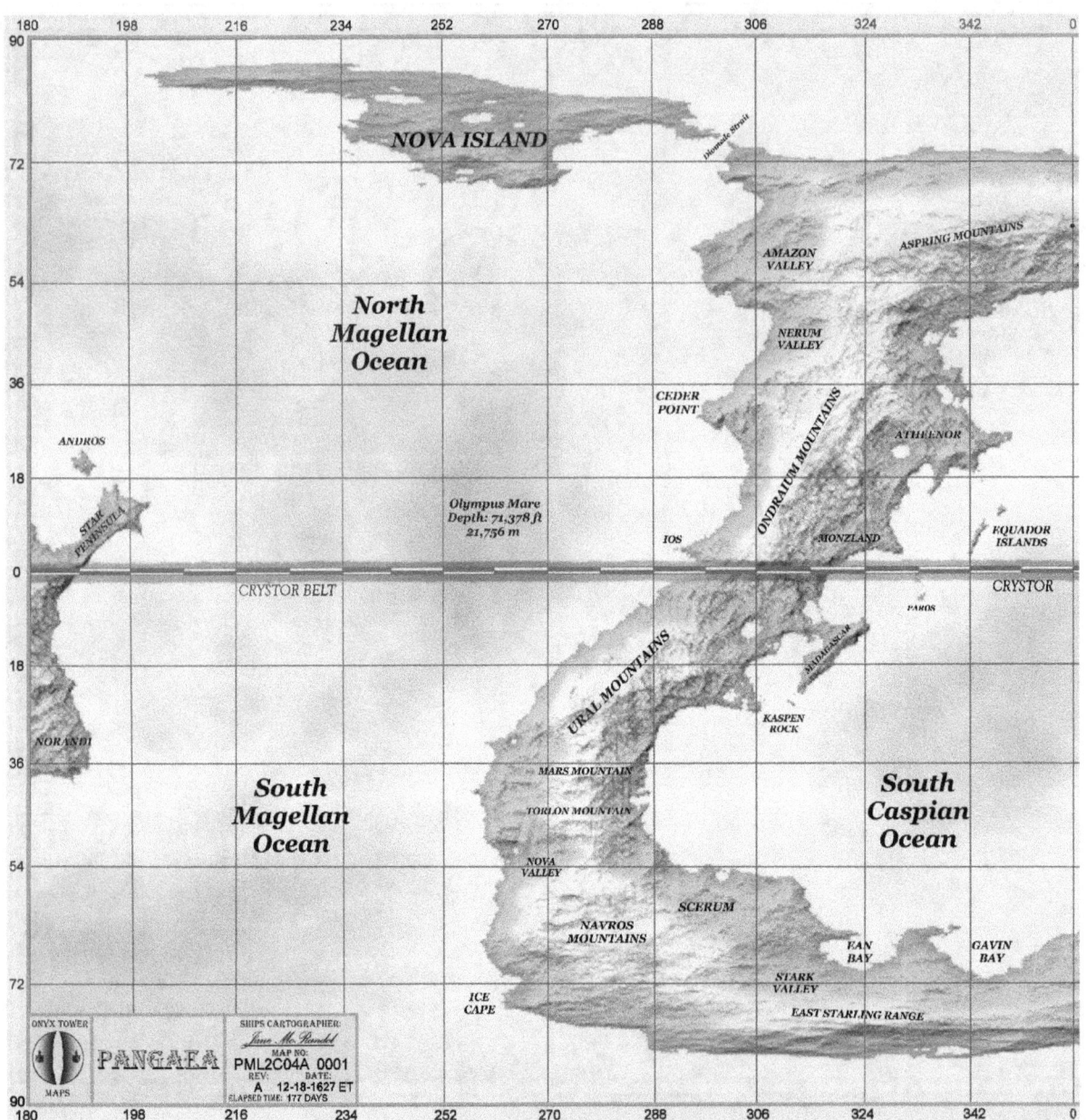

13. WHAN LIONHEART REVEALED AN EARLY MAP OF PANGARA, everyone was amazed at its detail and wondered about the depth of the captain's dreams as they all studied it closely. An updated version is shown above.

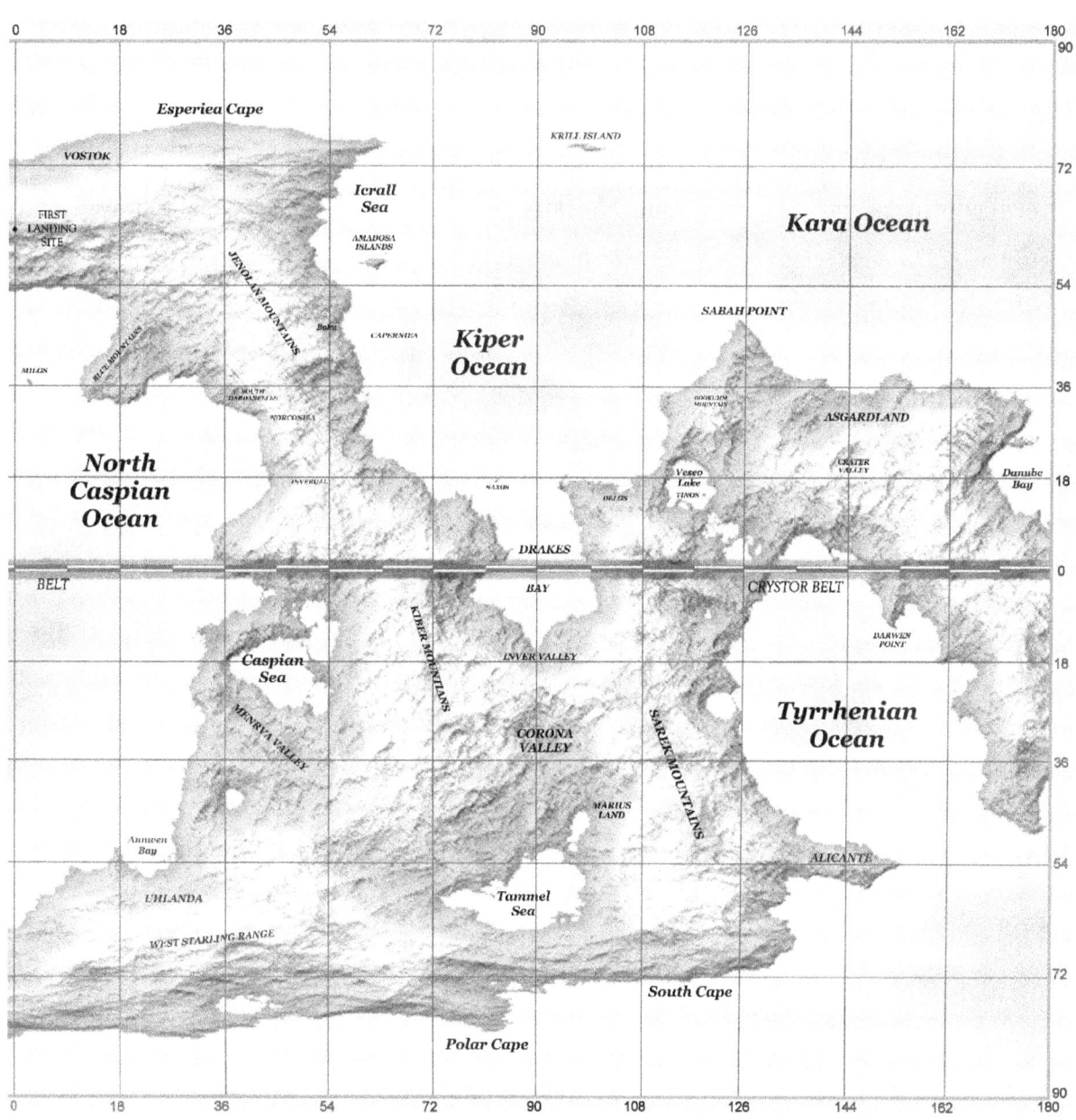

"Captain, I have more detailed information on the three areas of interest, but before we discuss them, I am curious to know what your dreams revealed regarding our trinary star system," West said.

"According to Argosh, we are in the Triausolees [Try-aus-so-leez] trinary star system. The star systems that make it up are Tiberium [Ti-beer-e-um], Saterium [Sat-ter-e-um], and Plutarius [Plu-tar-us]. Or at least it was until the Plutarius sun went nova several centuries ago. Pangaea orbits the Tiberium star. The Triausolees system, home to three stars was also home to three intelligent races. They were the tavin, the noelight [noel-light], and human. At that point, Argosh revealed he was of the tavin race," Lionheart said.

"Captain, one of the races was human?" Connors asked.

"Yes, Argosh said humans occupied this world and it's red sister planet long ago. They also had other settlements scattered throughout the Tiberium system. This double planet system was once home to a branch of the human race. By the time the first tavin arrived here, they discovered only the ancient remains of the human civilization. As far as the tavin could determine, the human race came to a sudden end long ago. They all vanished, leaving only their ruins behind. The tavin believe what came upon them may have been something like the black oil cloud of death that was circling this planet when we first arrived," Lionheart said.

"What were the tavin like?" Petrov asked.

"From what I could gather, the tavin look very much like humans physically, except their life span is longer. They seem more in tune with each other, and they are more in tune with nature. My dream left me with the impression they seek to live in harmony with nature, unlike humans who generally seek to conquer it," Lionheart said.

"The fall of humans, when did all this happen? What did they call this planet?" Connors asked.

"Argosh said the humans died out thousands of years ago. When the tavin first arrived, they were able to, at least in part, learn a little of human history by the ruins left behind. They called this world Pangaea, its energy moon Crystor and the red sister planet was called Torlon."

"Pangaea," Connors quietly said.

After giving everyone a moment to study the maps McRandel created, Lionheart continued. "Back on Earth there are some who believe that humans didn't originate there. Some believe they came from the stars. Some of the ruins we have examined on this planet are much older than any back on Earth. When Argosh told me about this, I wondered about the possibility that the people here might have reached the Earth in ancient times."

As Lionheart spoke, it suddenly occurred to him, when the crew was first considering names for this world, it was West who suggested the name Pangaea. Lionheart knew West had instant access to all recorded human history. He also wondered if West knew the real definition of Pangaea was not of a super continent on the Earth in an earlier time, but rather another Earthlike world.

"So, both the human and Tavin were in the same trinary star system, but ironically they never made direct contact," Thornton said.

"In my dream, I learned of stories and legends among the Tavin that told of isolated instances where humans visited the Tavin world in early times, but none ever tried to settle there. There is a theory that the Noelights may have intervened in some way to protect the Tavin species. If the humans had occupied their world, it is very likely they would have driven the Tavin into extinction.", Lionheart said.

"Why would you say that?" Connors asked.

"I hate to say this, but it has always been our nature. When there were two different species of humans on the Earth at one time, one drove the other into extinction. I'm referring to the Cro-Magnon and the Neanderthal," Lionheart said.

"Did you learn anything more about the Noelights?" West asked.

Argosh said the Noelights are much older and more advanced then the Human or Tavin. Their home planet was in what is now the green Plutarius nebula. Now, its planets are flung out into space. But there is an aspect of the Plutarius nova the Tavon can't explain," Lionheart said.

"What do you mean?" West asked.

"Argosh said Plutarius went nova thousands of years ago yet the position of its planets and exploded gas cloud suggest the event happened much more recently. It is as though time in that star system's proximity has slowed down. I told Argosh we encountered a planet from the Plutarius system when we first arrived here. It was a gas giant with a glowing green atmosphere filled with yellow lightning. Argosh said the planet we encountered is called Delcone [Dell-cone] and the moon we landed on was Delcone Three. He went on to say, Delcone was once in the third orbit of the Plutarius system, on the hot edge of what we refer to the habitable zone. The Tavin know very little about the Plutarius system. They were able to map it, but only from a distance. They sent ships there in past times, but none ever returned. The Tavin believe the Plutarius nebula may have been the result of a civil war between the Noelights. When it was going on, their spherical, black ships were seen everywhere. During that time, the Tavin recorded many explosions that were on a planetary scale throughout the Plutarius system," Lionheart said, pausing for a moment.

"In my dream, I told Argosh about the ship we discovered. I told him we detected a signal coming from a shipwreck on Delcone Three. The ship itself was spherical. Almost every surface inside and out had scratch marks. It looked as though something had successfully clawed its way in. I also told him we discovered what we thought was a forest of trees close by, but the trees turned out to be formations that consisted of an obsidian glass like material. I told him when we arrived at Pangaea and came under attack, West transmitted the same signal that came from the ship on Delcone Three and the attacking entity broke up into fragments and returned to the surface of

Pangaea. Once there, those fragments formed into a black forest like the one discovered near the shipwreck," Lionheart said.

"How did Argosh respond?" West asked.

He said the wreck we discovered was a Noelight ship and the entity that attacked was actually intended to terraform Pangaea. I also learned a similar entity came to the Tavin world over 26 centuries ago. It came in the form of a meteor shower that rained down on the entire planet. Once the meteors cooled, they cracked open revealing an oil-like substance that formed into black monsters. They tore into the Tavin population. They killed only Tavin, only intelligent life. The Tavin astronomers were able to trace the meteors origin back to Plutarius," Lionheart said.

"What happened then?" Connors asked.

"I don't know. Argosh only said there would be more if all went well. I have no idea what that means, although I believe it is somehow related to what I saw happening to the tower in my first dream and the three keys I need to open some sort of doorway. West did the survey reveal unusual atmospheric anomalies at the three areas of interest?" Lionheart asked.

"Several areas of similar temperatures to Crystor's Gate Island have been detected, however there is a strong possibility the atmospheric conditions in the areas of interest are natural. There is no real way to know without going there. Crystor's Gate Island would not have been discovered if it were not for the fact that the temperature changed at regular intervals," West said.

"I see. Thoughts anyone?" Lionheart asked.

"I don't know. Under normal conditions, your dreams might be a little farfetched, but after what has happened on this voyage so far, I think anything is possible. I'm talking about that calling card you left for your future self on Proxima b," Thornton said.

"Captain, you said you had three dreams. What was the third one about?" Petrov asked.

"This is where it gets interesting. Argosh said the coming of the Onyx Tower was foretold by a legend that started nearly a thousand years ago. He said the tower's second arrival will mark the end of the death cloud. Then he went on to say the tower's first coming will mark the return of humans to Pangaea," Lionheart said.

Captains Log: Our voyage elapsed time is now 173days (Dec 14th, 1627, Earth Time)

03:00 Hours:

It has been nearly a day since revealing my dreams to the senior officers. I think they believe me, at least for now. Since the meeting, West revealed there were unusual, small atmospheric disturbances detected on board our rotorcraft when we returned from the ruin site of Crystor's Gate. West later detected the same disturbances aboard the ship, most notably in my cabin. Based on those readings, West suggested something I would have quickly dismissed if it had come from anyone else. Put simply, West thinks we were not alone when we returned from the site. She thinks an entity was with us and is now aboard this ship. West also thinks this entity was able to communicate with me through my dreams. I avoid using the word "ghost".

Peter M Lionheart, Captain

AMADOSA

Captains Log: Our voyage elapsed time is now 175 days (Dec 16th, 1627, Earth Time)

05:30 Hours:

I had another dream which I don't plan to reveal to anyone. As before, it began with me standing in the moonlit garden at my aunt Fern's home and once again I approached her back door. As I looked closer at the three-lock box on the door, a white light came from the top keyhole. Looking into it, the area around me turned white. I was standing on a cold island, covered with snow and ice. It was calm at first, then I saw what looked like distant rocks slowly moving down the icy slope in my direction. As the rocks got closer, I could see they had legs and were not rocks at all, but rather large, bug like creatures. There was just a few at first, then they began to multiply and soon there were thousands of them. They were the approximate size of a big dog. I heard a crackling sound, as they got closer. I suddenly heard Argosh saying; "The key you seek is on this island, but you are in danger until the queen awakens." At that point, several of my crew approached from behind and started firing at the bugs. There was no stopping the creatures. For everyone killed, several more would appear. They just kept coming. I woke up swinging. Somehow, I know this place was related to Amadosa. Based in that dream or vision, I have decided the northern islands of Amadosa would be our first port of call. We should be there in a few hours.

Peter M Lionheart, Captain

14. CAPTAIN LIONHEART'S DREAMS were becoming so powerful he quietly revealed to Dr. Conners and West that he was almost afraid to go to sleep. In his latest dream he knew they had to visit the island of Amadosa, but it was also a very dangerous place.

The Onyx Tower dropped out of space into the skies over the Amadosa Islands. The location was so far north, the mid-day sun was only as bright as late afternoon. Before selecting a landing site, two rotorcraft were dispatched to survey the area. The largest island had the general shape of a handgun aimed to the west. It was 350 miles [563.3 Kilometers] wide and 290 miles [466.7 Kilometers] north to south. The island was a mix of green tundra with a rocky, snow covered range that ran from its western peninsula, across the top and on down to its southern peninsula. The area of the island where the gun's trigger would be was dominated by a large valley of rolling tundra. There were ruins from an ancient settlement in the valley's northwest area. The valley was filled with large elephant sized animals grazing on the tundra. Lionheart launched two drones to investigate the ruins, but when they were both destroyed by intense sonic waves generated by the creatures Lionheart ordered the two rotorcraft to keep their distance. The large herbivore creatures seemed peaceful if left alone, but their ability to focus deadly sonic waves at any possible threat made it clear that they dominated the area. Lionheart knew the bug creatures he saw in his vision were not on the big island below. He knew the sonic creatures could easily shatter them in an instant. West and Lionheart decided to move on.

The other islands of Amadosa were mostly rock and ice. The largest of them was located northeast of the main island. It was the crater of an extinct volcano approximately 50 miles [80.5 Kilometers] in diameter. There was an opening on the southern side where the crater wall had collapsed. It was the only part of the island that was flat near the shore. When Lionheart reviewed the survey, he recognized it from his dream. Ship's geologist, Flora Bascom, determined the flat area near the shore was the floor of an ancient lava bed that formed when the volcano's wall collapsed. The opening in the crater wall gave the island a horseshoe appearance. Several lava tube openings in the island's interior were clearly visible. Bascom also determined the island group was still active with geo-thermal activity. A large column of steam was misting out of the ocean, approximately three miles northwest. As the rotorcrafts flew in closer, they could see an abundance of ocean plant life growing in the warm waters surrounding the steam column. Flying even closer, a faint light became visible from the underwater heat source.

15. **THE LARGE VALLEY OF ROLLING TUNDRA** on Amadosa's main island was dominated by massive creatures that were capable of focusing powerful sonic energy. Having obliterated the two drones sent from the Onyx Tower, Lionheart ordered his two rotorcraft to keep their distance.

Lionheart had the Onyx Tower land halfway between the island and the warm water area. After meeting with his officers in the Wardroom, it was decided two landing parties would be dispatched. The first one consisted of two rotorcraft that would land at the south end on the flat shoreline. Lionheart would lead the party as they made their way into the crater of the extinct volcano. Petrov would lead the second landing party in an amphibian to explore the warm water northwest of the island. Survey images of the undersea light revealed luminous hot crystals that turned out to be the source of the steam column.

After flying low over the area, Lionheart decided to land the closer to the crater wall than originally intended. The other rotorcraft landed seconds later.

"Based on the dreams I had, I know I'm supposed to retrieve a key of some kind, but I don't have any idea exactly what I'm looking for," Lionheart said to West as he stepped out of the first rotorcraft.

"I suspect the object will be something obvious. A physical key in the typical sense is unlikely, but if the doorway you described in your dream was accurate, this key will unlock or influence an enormous amount of energy," West said, following Lionheart.

"What are you saying?" Lionheart ask as he turned around.

"If the doorway is a portal or a time storm like the ones we've encountered, a vast amount of energy is needed to create them. So far, the only physical object that can influence that level of energy would be in a crystal form of some kind," West said.

"Like the formations that line the interior of Crystor?" Lionheart asked.

"Precisely. I would suggest the object we are looking for is a stone crystal of some kind, one that is capable of conducting extreme levels of energy," West said, looking up at the crater walls. Something seemed out of place. There were large, smooth boulders, thousands of them everywhere. Preliminary scans revealed their mineral composition differed from the volcanic crater.

Alexi Ivanov Personal log: Our voyage elapsed time is now 176 days (Dec 17th, 1627, Earth Time)

In the interest of carrying out the Guardian's request to deliver a vial to the Amadosa queen, I volunteered to go with Petrov's party to investigate the undersea area north of the main island. Upon reaching the "hot crystals" (as they were later called), it was clear they were the sole source of heat that made this tropical marine oasis possible, even in the cold northern waters of Pangaea. Petrov believes the crystals are not natural. After examining their formation, Petrov had the amphibian circle the site in a slow outward spiral. We discovered a current of warm water leading out of the area. It funneled into an undersea cave that led under the island. A dim, green light came from inside. The cave was large enough for the amphibian so Petrov decided to follow the flow of warm water as far as he could. The dim light we saw came from luminescent stones all around. The cave opening led into a large cavern network that ran beneath the island.

It was hard to estimate the distance traveled, but we discovered a beachhead, approximately two miles into the cave's interior. We came up on the beach and stepped out of the amphibian. The air was breathable. A mist rising from the warm seawater made the cave's air misty. There were large, elongated, smooth rocks everywhere. To our surprise and horror, they turned out to be large, flesh eating insects. We later called them ice beetles. Before we could react, they blocked our path back to the amphibian. Then they herded us into a central area that surrounded a steamy pool of water. The security crew opened fire on them in an effort to get back. The ice beetles exploded under the force of their electric pulse rifles, but more and more beetles kept coming. When the rifles were depleted, the beetles attacked, devouring the two who fired on them. The beetles herded the remaining four of us back into the pool chamber. Once there, they retreated to the chamber's entrance, blocking the only way out. Their behavior suggested they were under the influence of someone or something. I started to feel we were not going to be devoured.

After my fear subsided, I began to look around the chamber. It was dark. The glow of green stones in the pool was the main source of light. I held my lantern up to see more clearly. My cold fear returned when I saw the countless human and animal skeleton fragments imbedded in the icy floor and walls all around. The beetles seemed almost passive as they continued to block the only exit. They closed ranks and hissed at Petrov when he stepped in their direction. I recall hearing of insect species that bring captured food to their queen.

Something was moving in the pool. The steamy mist over murky water made it hard to see. We saw only a dark shadowy form at first, but as it got closer to the surface, the upper part of it appeared human. She rose out of the water, stopping just above her waist. She looked human in general form only. Her skin was like smooth, black porcelain with white markings on her face, chest and shoulders. Not saying a word, she carefully studied our faces. I will never forget those black, stone-like eyes when she looked at me. When she came up out of the pool, we could see she was only half-human. The bottom half of her body was that of a large black insect, like a wingless wasp. All of us became frozen in fear as she slowly stepped closer. There was no expression on her face. I had the overwhelming feeling she wanted to eat us. I wondered which one of us she would pick first. At that moment, I remembered the vial the Guardian had given me, and his instructions to give it to the queen. As she came closer to look me over, I held it out to her. Her cool tone changed as she took the vial from my hand.

Breaking the silence, she began speaking slowly revealing herself as Isis, fifth daughter of Lance, the first queen of Amadosa. I later learned Isis had been in hibernation for centuries, waiting for Lionheart's arrival. She asked Petrov if he was Lionheart. When Petrov revealed Lionheart was leading a landing party up on the surface, Isis looked over at the ice beetles and motioned her head slightly. None of us knew, but at that very moment the beetle attack on Lionheart's party stopped. We later learned his party had come under attack shortly after they first landed. West was the first to detect the ice beetles because their shells were slightly warmer than the surrounding rocks. The fighting had escalated to the point where the Onyx Tower came to rain down lightning on the hordes of attacking beetles.

16. PETROV'S LANDING PARTY ENCOUNTERS QUEEN ISIS in the deep undersea cave of what later became known as Amadosa's Queens Island.

Alexi Ivanov Personal log: Our voyage elapsed time is now 177 days (Dec 18th, 1627, Earth Time)

It is clear that Queen Isis had some kind of direct mental link with the ice beetles. She was able to stop the attack without saying a word. She later met with Lionheart on the surface. During their meeting, in a somewhat joking manner, she asked Lionheart to forgive her pets, saying they can be a little unruly around visitors. Isis told Lionheart she was expecting his arrival and presented him with what looked like a crystal sphere. I didn't get a good look, but it appeared to have a diameter of approximately 15 inches [381mm] and there was a small pulsing point of light at the center of it. I had the impression the sphere contained a small star.

As dangerous as the smaller island "Queens Island" (as it is now called) was, the larger island would have been instantly fatal to anyone landing there. It is inhabited by large, grass-eating creatures that can kill by creating an intense sonic cone directed at the threat. Lionheart decided not to explore it after several probes disintegrated shortly after collecting images of these creatures. I suspect even Isis is afraid of them.

The encounter at Amadosa revealed two things. First, there is a very good chance that if we encounter any people, they will know of us, because at some point the tower and its crew are going to go back in time to create history. Second, I was fascinated to encounter a half-human. I don't know how Isis came to be, but the prospect of a hybrid creature opens some interesting historical possibilities. I am delighted at the possibility of creating horrifying legends. I understand why the Guardian arranged for me to be with the tower's crew at this time.

17. THE MEETING LIONHEART HAD WITH QUEEN ISIS was one he never expected. The energy key he received was more or less what he and West anticipated, but what caught him by surprise was that Isis was only half human. When Lionheart went through the regeneration to extend his life, he always wondered what would happen if an animal entered the isolated chamber during the process. Queen Isis was living proof that this had happened sometime in the past. He quietly wondered if it had been accidental or intentional.

Having completed their mission, the Onyx Tower lifted off. Lionheart looked out over the snow-covered islands of Amadosa as the tower ascended. He had the first key, but it came at a terrible price. The beetle attack on his landing party cost the lives of six crewmembers and West sustained heavy damage. The beetle attack left both rotorcrafts so badly damaged they had to be lifted back into the tower by balloon crane.

After seeing Isis, Lionheart continued to wonder about the danger that would eventually come to pass, the existence of hybrid animal-humans. He knew it was one of the darker possibilities that came with the re-generation pods the ship was carrying. If a person went through re-generation alone, the process would go as planned. If that person was with someone or something, the new re-generated life form would be a hybrid of the two. At this point it was clear that Isis was once a crewmember or the descendant of a crewmember that went through the process with an insect of some kind. Lionheart also realized another side effect is that the hybrid seems to have influence over animals of the same species that it formed with. It was another cause for worry.

After Lionheart had gone through the regeneration process himself, he knew he had become only half human. His plant side would greatly extend his life span. But there was another side to it. It was a side he never considered until now. After regeneration, Lionheart recalled taking time off to be in the woods to relax and commune with nature. He remembered the wonderful feeling of being able to sense the life force of the plants and trees around him. At the time he thought he was just happy to be alive and young again, but now he realized it was something more, something much more. When a person goes through regeneration, they form a strong psychic bond with the foreign entity of their new body. Even though Lionheart knew there was a history of human-animal hybrids, he ordered the re-generation pods placed under tighter security.

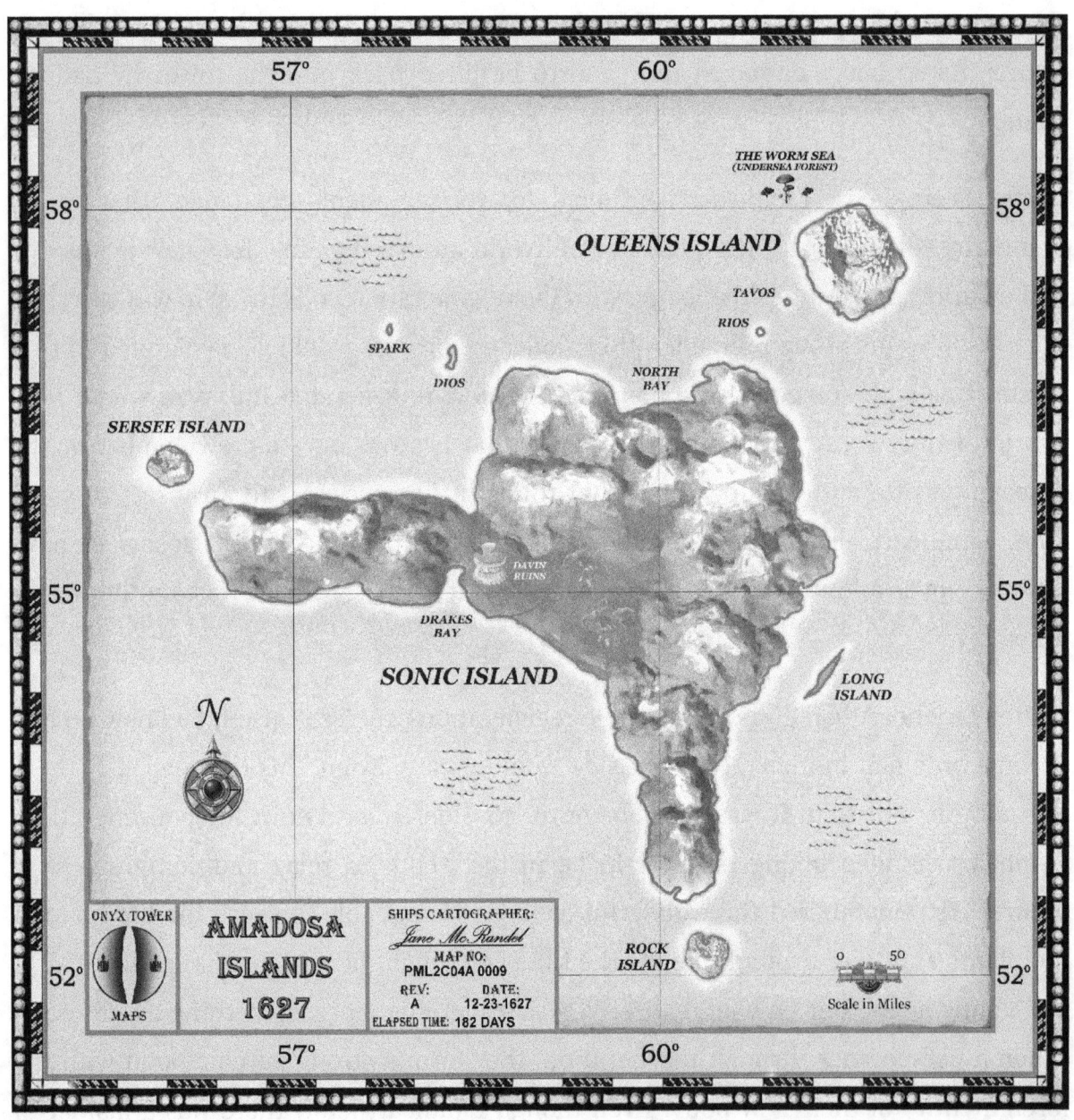

18. **A MAP OF THE AMADOSA ISLANDS** was later rendered by ship's head cartographer, Jane McRandel.

CAPERNIEA

Having received the small sphere of energy from Isis, Lionheart had Petrov construct a safe enclosure for it and secure it down in engineering. The order was given for the tower to hold altitude at 1000 feet [304.8m] and head slowly south. He was still deeply saddened and disturbed by the loss of six crew members. Lionheart wanted time to console with their friends and loved ones while holding services before reaching their next destination even though Lionheart wasn't certain what that next destination would be. He also felt a slow course would allow him time to rest.

Lionheart returned to his quarters after services. Alone in his cabin, he drifted off into a deep sleep, but just before drifting off completely, he thought he heard a faint sound of tinkling crystals. The "Battle of the Ice Beetles" (as it was later known), left him exhausted. A small, luminescent creature scarcely four inches long, appeared hovering over his desk. Its dark blue silk, fish-like body tapered down to a thin, pink tale. It slowly moved its luminous green, bat like wings as though it were underwater. Two long, black antennas with glowing orange tips, extended out of its head. The tiny sparkles of yellow light around the creature gave it a fairy like appearance. Aside from the faint sound of tinkling crystals, it flew around the cabin in almost complete silence. It flew over to Lionheart, hovering above him as he slept.

Submerged once again in a deep dream state, Lionheart found himself back in Kensington Park, London, outside the home of his Aunt Fern. It was a dark night. Just as before, he stood in the garden behind her home. As he stepped closer to the back door, he could see the three-lock box. This time there was a key in the top keyhole. As he leaned in closer, a faint blue light came out of the second keyhole. It became brighter as he got closer. He knelt down to look straight into it. As before, the keyhole was like a small opening to an outside world. Lionheart strained to look closer. The light from the second keyhole grew brighter until he found himself standing on the coast of an island under the noon sun. Lionheart was reminded of Star Island, the first site on Pangaea the crew members visited. Looking around, Lionheart saw the great white amphibian creatures coming and going from the egg nest at the island's center. He had the overwhelming feeling Argosh was somewhere nearby. Something about the island was different from what he remembered. He looked down at his feet and saw human footprints in the sand. The bare footprints led into the sea.

The next thing he knew he was out in the water, looking back at the island. The water washed over him as he sank below the surface. He took a sudden breath at first, then his breathing returned to normal even though he was now underwater. Lionheart started moving away from the island. As he got further out, he was going deeper. He sensed there was a deep canyon ahead that had tall vertical monoliths, towering far above the canyon floor. Lionheart saw dim, yellow stars floating on the rocky formations of the sea floor. Moving in closer the stars became the lights of a city. Lionheart had the feeling he wasn't alone. It suddenly dawned on him that he was in the shadow of something above. It was very large and closing on his position. He took a deep gasp for air and woke up. At the very moment he opened his eyes, he thought a dim light had gone out in his cabin.

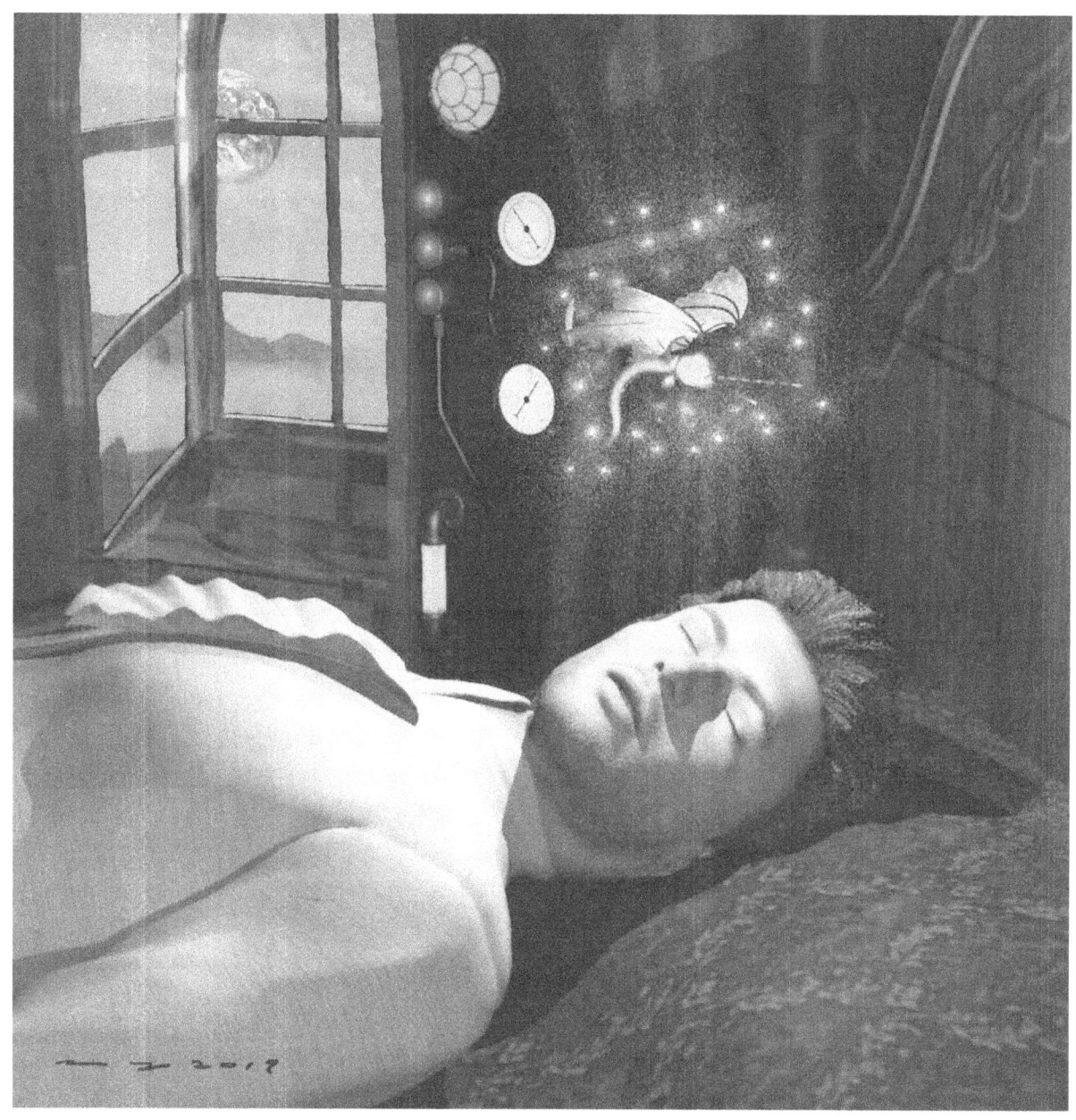

19. AS LIONHEART SLEPT, the entity of Argosh continued to reach into his dreams.

20. **SUBMERGED IN A DEEP DREAMSTATE,** Lionheart once again found himself in the moonlit garden of his Aunt Fern's home. As he approached the back door, he saw a key in the top lock of the three lock box. As lionheart looked closer at the bright blue light coming from the second lock hole, he soon found himself in the undersea world of what would be their next destination, Caperniea.

Caperniea would be their next destination. Lionheart waited until West was fully repaired before holding another meeting in the wardroom. Before the meeting, he looked over several maps McRandel created, hoping to be more definite about their next destination. He had an idea of the general location he dreamt of. It was somewhere directly south of Amadosa. "That's it!", he yelled as he saw a map with an island marked "Triton Island" on it.

Everyone was aware Lionheart knew where their next destination would be before the meeting. The table in front of them was covered with maps and images of an area in the Icrall Sea, directly south of Amadosa. As he pointed out Triton Island, they noticed the physical similarity to Star Island, they visited earlier.

"I had my curiosity about Star Island," West said, looking at some of the images.

"What do you mean?" Lionheart asked.

"I suspected the dome like nest cave at the islands center was not natural. Someone wanted the Great Whites to nest there. I knew sooner or later, we would get back there to investigate further or investigate one similar," West said.

"I had another dream. I dreamt I was on another island similar to Star Island. In my dream, I saw human footprints that led into the sea. There is something out there in the deep water. West, do we have any information on the undersea terrain in this area?" Lionheart asked.

"So far we have only a general overlay of Pangaea's ocean floors," West said as she sifted through some of the images.

"I'm interested to see if there is any deep water near this island," Lionheart said.

West pulled an image of a distant view of the island showing much of the surrounding ocean. "Most of the island has a shallow runoff into the sea, except here," she said pointing to the area south. "In this area, there is a steep drop-off that appears to be the edge of a canyon. We also detected several steep monolith structures that almost reach the surface," she said.

"Yes," Lionheart quietly said to himself as he looked at the image.

"Captain, I also wondered about what we found on Star Island. If someone created a breeding ground for these Great White creatures, why would they do it? I would think the Great Whites would be too dangerous," Thornton said.

"They have the physical means to be, however, unlike the Great White sharks of Earth, the amphibious Great Whites here are highly intelligent. When the first landing party came under attack by a yellow worm, the Great Whites collectively herded it into the water before devouring it. Their behavior suggests that they hunt in packs. Based on my observation, I believe they have an intelligence similar to a killer whale and as such may be trainable," West said, interrupting Lionheart.

"Do you mean they can be trained like a horse?" Petrov asked.

"I only suggest some domestication may be possible based on what we observed. You will note, the only interest they had in the landing party occurred when one of their eggs had been stolen by a party member. Once the egg was recovered, they lost interest in the party. I'm suggesting if there are inhabitants living here under the sea, they may have a relationship with the Great Whites in some way." West said.

"I guess will find out soon enough. We should arrive at the island in a couple of hours," Lionheart said.

At Triton Island, it was another bright sunny day as the clouds rolled across the sky in the early afternoon. The light of day became dark as the Onyx Tower descended from the clouds, casting its shadow across the island. The tower set down off the island's southwest coast. A short time later, an amphibian from the tower came up out of the waves on to the island's only beach that wasn't swampy. Reaching dry sand, it stopped. The area was quiet. There were no great whites or yellow worms around. The top hatch opened. Lionheart, West, Holston, and a heavily armed Mullin came out and stood on the sand. Lionheart stepped away, looking down at all the tracks left by the great whites. He saw only their footprints at first. Then he saw other prints. It was just as in his dream. The bare human footprints were unmistakable.

"Curious." West said kneeling down to get a closer look. "Is this what you saw in your dream?" she asked.

"Yes, it's part of it. I want to see if there is any truth to the rest of my dream," Lionheart said as he stood up and got back on the amphibian.

With everyone back on board, the amphibian returned to the sea and submerged. Lionheart steered the craft in the same general direction of his dream. At first, he ran shallow at a depth of 20 feet. It wasn't much further until their sonar detected the monoliths ahead. Following the direction of his dream, Lionheart increased his depth to 40 feet. At that depth, the afternoon sun still enabled them to see a hundred yards. The monoliths were still beyond their view. They could only see blue water ahead. Then something appeared on the forward port side. They could see only a vague, dark outline. It turned in front of them. Now it was moving away, following the same course.

"West?" Lionheart asked.

"Sonar has detected a great white, but the profile is different. There seems to be something on its back. It is directly ahead," West said.

"I want to get a closer look," Lionheart said as he increased speed slightly.

"Sonar has detected other great whites entering the area behind us. The one ahead could be part of a school," West said.

The great white ahead came into better view as they got closer. It had something unusual secured to the animal's back. It was starting to descend.

21. AS LIONHEART AND WEST pursued the submerged great white, they could see it had something attached to its back.

"What the hell is that?" Mullin quietly asked.

"It almost looks like a brown sack of potatoes with a forward glass eye," Lionheart said as he maneuvered the amphibian above it." The glass eye was actually a transparent dome allowing the human pilot inside to steer the animal underwater. Lionheart couldn't believe what he was seeing.

"Interesting. It would seem the people living here have mastered a way of life under the sea," West said with no expression.

Lionheart was completely captivated by what he was seeing. Something pulled West's attention away from the window. Sonar detected two great whites closing from behind, just above them. There were faint echoes of something between them. Before she could warn Lionheart, they lunged downward on each side, capturing the amphibian in a net.

"What the hell-," Lionheart said as the net came down over the window.

West detected two more great whites coming up on each side of the stern. The controls no longer responded. "Dammit," Lionheart said as the amphibian's propeller jammed. The nets holding the amphibian began to tighten. Lionheart shut the engine down to avoid overheating. The thought of blowing ballast crossed his mind, but then his mission was to make contact with the Capernieans. Being captured wasn't what he had in mind.

"Interesting. The thought never occurred to me, but it makes perfect sense," West said.

"West?" Lionheart asked.

"I was thinking of our making contact with anyone on this planet who managed to evade the death cloud. It never occurred to me that if they had sufficient safeguards in place, there is a good chance that our first contact would result in our capture," West said.

22. BEFORE HE COULD REACT, Lionheart's amphibian finds itself surrounded by manned great whites.

"Well, I suppose this is better than being attacked by ice beetles," Mullin said.

"Captain, I suggest we adjust our ballast accordingly to wherever they are taking us. They may be as curious about us as we are about them. The Onyx Tower may also be part of their history, just as it was for the Amadosa," West said.

"You may be right. Inform the tower of our situation," Lionheart said.

"I'm unable to do that. When they jammed our propeller, the trailing antenna was severed," West said.

Lionheart didn't say anything. Despite his uneasiness, he had an inescapable feeling, he was right where he should be.

"Look," Mullin said as several yellow lights up ahead came into view.

They were deeper now. The faint outline of the surrounding monoliths could now be seen. Even though it was a bright sunny day above, the warm glowing lights in their dark underwater surroundings had the look of a deep forest village at night. The great whites pulled the amphibian into one of the larger cave openings. Lionheart strained to see the yellow underwater lights that illuminated the cave. The lights were clearly some form of luminescent rock. The cave led upward then forward again. They entered what looked like a grand sunken temple. It's Greek styled features made Lionheart think of Atlantis. The amphibian came to rest on the flat stone surface of the temple floor. With the net still wrapped around the amphibian, the great whites departed. Despite his uncertainty, Lionheart marveled at the temple's glass columns all around. They were filled with bubbling water. There were openings in the temple walls beyond, each revealing stairs leading up. A large air pocket started to form above them. As the water surface got lower, they realized it would soon drain from the temple completely.

"If this keeps up we should be able to open the hatch in a few minutes," Mullin said.

"Interesting, the outside pressure indicates we are on the surface," West said.

"How can that be? No islands were detected in this area," Lionheart said.

23. **THE SUNKEN TEMPLE CAVE BECAME BRIGHTER** as the water drained out. After it was drained, sunlight came from the top of the stairways all around. Shadows appeared on all of them.

"It looks like we are about to meet the Capernieans," Lionheart said.

Moments later, several people entered the temple and stood all around the amphibian. Lionheart didn't know what to make of their dress. They looked like a culture that was somewhere between ancient Egypt and Rome. Dr. Holsten, the ships anthropologist, was amazed. He was convinced they had encountered a true Atlantean, under sea culture. Some of the larger males got up on the amphibian and removed the netting. Afterward, they got down and stood with the others, nodding at one who appeared to be the leader. The leader looked more like a king with his crown. A tall, striking woman stood close by his side. There were two well-dressed men standing on each side them. One was dressed in white, the other in black.

"Well, we might as well go out and make contact with our captors, now that we have them right where they want us. Mullin, let's assume a friendly posture until the situation proves otherwise," Lionheart said.

"Understood," Mullin said as he holstered his weapon.

West was quiet. Lionheart wasn't sure how they were going to respond to a mechanical person.

"West?" Lionheart asked.

"I have my concerns Captain," West said.

"What do you mean?"

"I still haven't made contact with the ship. I have detected a field similar to one discovered at Crystor's Gate," West said.

"Well. We will try to find out soon enough," Lionheart said, as he opened the hatch.

One by one they came out of the amphibian and stood before the leader. Lionheart noticed the man dressed in white next to the women had deep green eyes and pointed ears. A feeling of deja vu came over Lionheart. He somehow knew the man was of the Tavin race and tried to conceal his reaction.

"I'm Captain Lionheart, this is my chief mechanical officer Ms. West, ships head anthropologist, Dr. Holsten and security officer Mr. Mullin. We came from my starship, the Onyx Tower."

Mention of the Onyx Tower caused a reaction. It was clear all of them heard the name before and it had special meaning. After looking at each other they turned their attention back to Lionheart's party. At first there was silence. Then the leader stepped forward and spoke.

"I am Marco, first citizen of Caperniea. This is Alexandra, first lady of Caperniea," he said motioning to the woman standing next to him. "This is Darius, chief of armed forces," Marco said motioning to the man dressed in black. "-and this is Alika, guardian of the legend key," Marco said motioning to the man in white, standing next to Alexandra. "Recently, when the black oil cloud of death failed to pass overhead at its regular interval, I knew the ancient legend had finally come to pass. Several among us were not surprised when the Onyx Tower came to our waters. The legend foretold of your coming. It said, the return of the tower will mark the end of the terrible curse that has plagued Pangaea for centuries. You are welcome here Captain," Marco said extending his hand in friendship. He looked at West's green glowing eyes. "Mrs. West, the legend told of you as well. It said there would be one among the tower's crew who's neither living nor dead and is of one mind with the tower. The power of electricity runs through you veins," Marco said pausing for a moment.

"Fascinating, I have heard of this power, but the use of it ended centuries ago when the black curse arrived. Please come," Marco said as he motioned to lead Lionheart's team out of the chamber.

24. **LIONHEART'S PARTY ENCOUNTERED** the undersea Caperniean race for the first time.

"In a manner of speaking, you are correct," West said.

Marco escorted Lionheart's party through a series of tunnels that led to a large chamber beneath the sea. Once there, they were seated at a large banquet table. Lionheart, Holsten, and Mullin were overwhelmed by the chamber's large, crystalline windows that boasted fantastic views of Caperniea's undersea world.

"We have watched you from the moment the tower arrived. You must be hungry from your journey. Let me show you the bountiful food the sea provides," Marco said as several men entered the chamber carrying trays of food.

"I'm impressed with your mastery over the sea," Lionheart said.

"The sea provides all our wants. There is nothing here of the land," Darius said as he took a helping of food.

"True enough Darius. We have become masters of the sea. Actually, our way of life was forced upon us. Living beneath the waves is the only thing that saved us from the cloud of death. Now that the curse that drove us beneath the sea has ended, we can return to the surface and live out in the open as we once did centuries ago," Marco stopped to take a deep breath. "We can return to Baku, the place that was once our homeland. We can rebuild the nation we once had."

"Was Baku your homeland?" Holsten asked.

"Baku was the coastal river valley at the edge of the Icrall sea. It was once the capital of Caperniea. What you see here is only a small part of a nation that once was," Marco said.

"Marco, I must admit your people have accomplished a great deal. From what I've seen, you have an extensive network of underwater caverns here. How did your people first discover them?" Lionheart asked.

"We didn't. We were led to them. Many centuries ago, Caperniea was a small thriving coastal nation, located at the mouth of the Antilles River. Our nation originally began as a fishing village by a group of Tavin and Human who fled from the Invergal Empire. Over time, we eventually won our independence. From the very beginning, there was a legend that said a time of judgement was coming to Pangaea. According to it, the time of darkness would be marked by the appearance of a bright, green cloud among the stars. It said Pangaea would be cleansed of all corruption brought on by the hybrids. The legend went on to say the end of judgement would be marked by the coming of an Onyx Tower from the stars," Macro said.

"Marco, who are the hybrids?" Lionheart asked.

"Hybrids are creatures that are neither man nor animal. According to the Tavin, they first appeared on Pangaea nearly a thousand years ago. They were powerful creatures who commanded plants or animals that were similar to their own being," Marco said.

"I don't understand," Lionheart said.

"The first known hybrid was Belinda. She was worshiped as a God who ruled over the Invergal Empire. She was said to be half human half snake and as such, had command over all snakes. In addition to a regular army, the Invergal Empire also had an army of snakes. They made her empire virtually impregnable. Her end was somewhat ironic," Marco said.

"What happened?" Holston asked.

"During a battle, she was swallowed whole by a dragon. The irony was she had the human-dragon hybrid created to increase her power over all people living beyond the borders of her empire. It was said, the beast turned on her because its human element was directly related to people in the underclass she had whipped and tortured."

"Captain, you asked about how this place was discovered. Not all hybrids were evil. After many years of freedom, the Capernieans eventually became masters of the sea.

The intelligent, amphibious great whites that once struck terror and fear into our people, were eventually domesticated. This enabled us to harvest the sea as never before," Marco said.

"Until coming to Caperniean waters, the great whites we encountered were considered very intelligent, powerful and dangerous. We had the strong impression such an animal could never be domesticated," Marco said.

"How was that possible?" Holston asked.

"It was possible only by way of the Sharkman," Marco replied.

"The Sharkman?" Lionheart asked.

"Yes, back in the early days when Caperniea was still a land faring nation, there was a legend that someday we would someday live in the undersea world. But, to do that we would have to form an alliance with one of the greatest of sea creatures, the great white. The stories of human-hybrid creatures began to spread a thousand years ago. Some of the stories led to the startup of cults. One of the cults started around a man who became a hybrid with the egg of a great white. He was humanoid in appearance with a strong powerful body, but he had the head of a great white. They called him the Sharkman," Marco said.

Everyone became quiet as Marco continued.

"It was said that even though Sharkman's appearance and deep voice was frightening, he was friendly. He was able to communicate with both humans and with great whites on a telepathic level. At first only he and he alone would approach the great whites. He made an alliance with them. In exchange for their friendly domestication, the Capernieans built the hollow dome mountain structures where the great whites could safely lay their eggs. The Capernieans also helped create areas to increase the harvest of yellow worms, a major food source for great whites." Marco said.

"This alliance the Sharkman made, is that when all this started?" Lionheart asked as he looked out at the undersea.

25. **THE SHARKMAN** makes the first direct contact with the great whites. He was able to form an alliance that would help make the Capernieans masters of the undersea world.

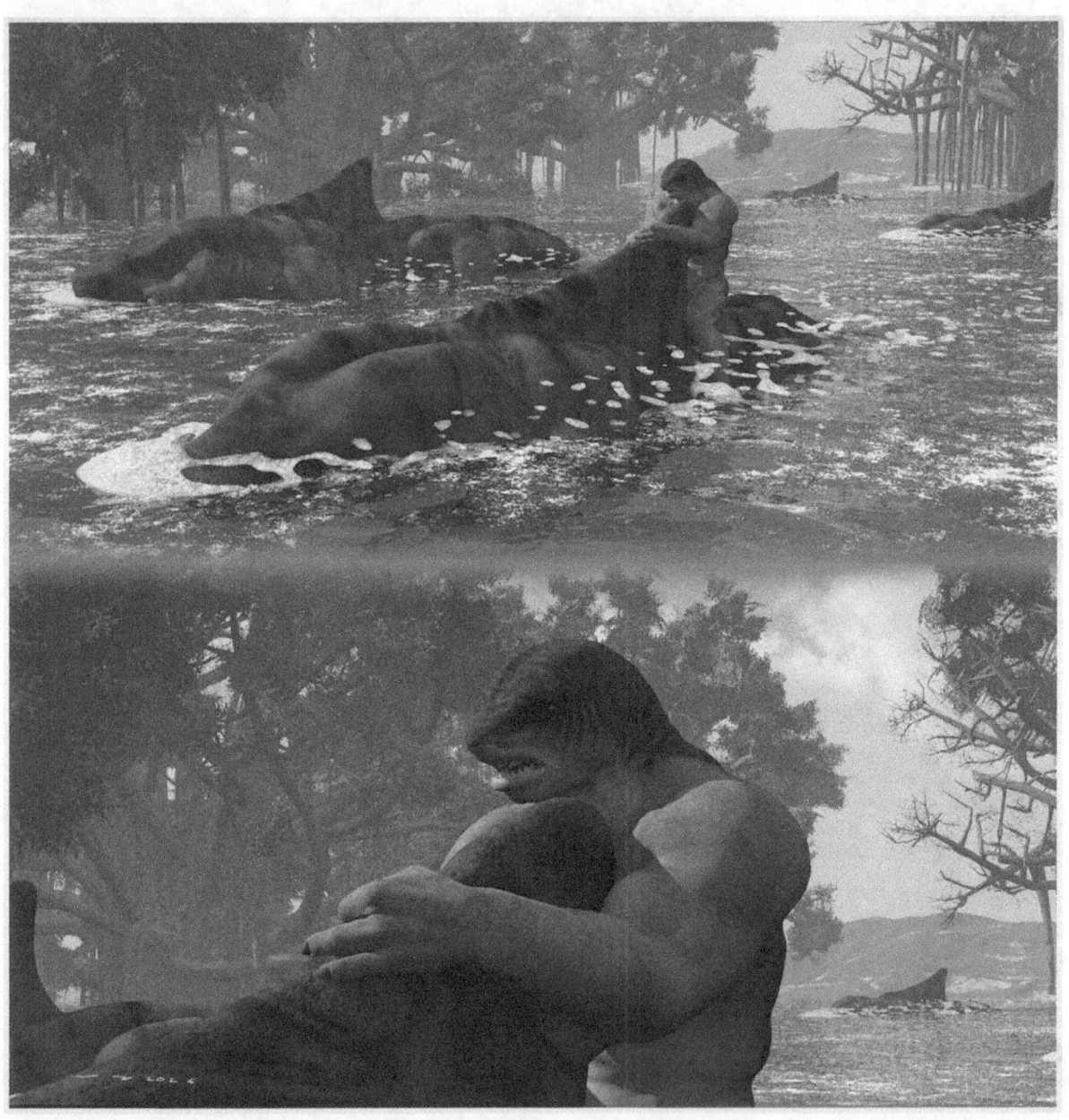

26. **HAVING MADE AN ALLIANCE** with the great whites, the Sharkman is shown the world beneath sea.

"No, it wasn't captain. Our life beneath the sea came years later. Sharkman's alliance enabled us to harvest beneath the sea, but we were still very much a landbound nation that lived at the seashore. We had sea faring ships but only a few worked with the great whites directly. It stayed that way for many years. In time, legends from the past began to fade. There was a small religious group among us who believed in the day of judgment that was to come. They believed to escape from it, we had to find a way not only to harvest, but live beneath the sea. About this time another hybrid from the sea appeared. He called himself Triton. He warned us of the day of judgement to come and led our people to this place. In the beginning, it was too dangerous to come here, but Triton had dominion over one of the most dangerous sea predators, the steel fish. Even the great whites are afraid of them. The steel fish are small fish that swim in large schools. They have sharp, stone like teeth that can chew through anything, even metal. Triton made it safe for us to come here. Without his influence, all Capernieans would have perished," Marco said.

"It must have taken a long time for the entire inhabitants of Caperniea to come here," Holston said.

"No, Doctor Holston. What you see here is only a part of Caperniea. When Triton first appeared, his presence stirred the people up. They thought he might be another hybrid from Invergal. They were also on edge because there was another legend that foretold a fish hybrid from the sea would come to save as many as he could before the judgement," Marco said.

Not saying anything, Lionheart looked over at West as Marco continued. "By the time Triton came to us, many believed the cloud of death was only a myth. They believed Triton was only trying to lure them away from Baku, so the Invergal or someone else could move in claim it. However, there were a few who believed Triton was sincere. They departed Baku in several ships and followed him across the Icrall Sea to this area."

"The cloud of death came shortly after the Plutarius nebula first appeared in the stars. Those who were still on the surface when the death cloud first arrived were torn to shreds. We learned later it was safe to come to the surface between intervals of the cloud's passing. Your presence and the absence of the cloud means the time of judgement has passed," Marco said.

27. TRITON, THE FISH-HUMAN HYBRID.

28. **IN A TIME BEFORE THE PLUTARIUS NEBULA,** Triton led the Capernieans who believed in the coming of the death cloud away from Baku and followed him across the Icrall sea to a place of safety.

"When we first came to Pangaea, we estimated Plutarius exploded approximately three and a half centuries ago. The earlier years before that would have been the approximate time when Triton first came here. What became of him?" Lionheart asked.

"Several decades after our arrival to this place beneath the sea, Triton disappeared. Despite his absence, many believed he was still around because the steel fish still protected us. Years later, Triton, or perhaps I should say, what was left of him, was discovered in the North Dardanelle Reef not far from here. He's became part of the reef itself. Triton is now more plant then animal," Marco said. Not saying anything, Lionheart looked at West. Marco continued. "You will see him soon enough. We know why you have come here. The key you seek is with Triton."

"The Key?" Lionheart asked.

"Yes Captain. In addition to the stories that told your arrival would mark the end of the death cloud, it also told of the three keys that would enable you to come here the first time," Marco said.

"I don't think I understand," Lionheart said.

"That's unfortunate, I was hoping you could explain it to me," Marco said.

"Captain, I'm registering an internal power loss. I need to return to the ship as soon as possible," West said.

"The key we have is with Triton. When you return, you can retrieve it from him. We will show you the way. Now, let me show you the way out. It will be more direct them the way you came in," Marco said.

29. AS MARCO LED LIONHEART'S PARTY back to the temple chamber they briefly stopped at a large viewing window that overlooked much of the undersea settlement. Lionheart was amazed at the Capernieans mastery of the sea.

A short time later, Lionheart's team returned to the temple. The netting had been removed from the amphibian. Once they were back on board, Marco motioned to one of his people and the temple wall in front of the amphibian began to open revealing the light of day. Looking through the nose window, Lionheart waved at Marco as they departed. As the amphibian rolled out of the temple and entered the water, Lionheart didn't submerge. The Onyx Tower was in plain view, several miles away. Once they were a short distance out, they looked back at the Caperniean temple. It was a large stone building, perched alone on a solitary rock, just above the water surface. The statues all around continued to remind Lionheart of Greek or Atlantean culture. Above the temple, was a stone sphere, supported by three columns. Lionheart realized the temple was under the same atmospheric shield as Crystor's Gate. Traveling further out, as they passed beyond the atmospheric barrier, West regained contact with the tower. Even though they were running on the surface, Lionheart could see he had a Caperniean escort of manned great whites all around, just below the waves.

Marco and his party stepped out into the temple roof and watched Lionheart departing.

"Do you think he will survive the test?" Alexandra asked.

"I don't know. So many have died. He will survive if he is the real Lionheart," Marco said.

"And if he doesn't?" Darius asked.

"If he is shredded, he will be the latest of the many imposters that tried to get the key. Still, the death cloud missed its regular interval for the first time in centuries. There is also that ship of his, the Onyx Tower. If the cloud was still active, I doubt his tower would have survived for long," Marco said.

"Either way, we will know soon enough,", Alika said.

30. **LIONHEARTS PARTY** departs from the Caperniean temple. The structure of Caperniea above the sea was only possible because of the protective field that kept it hidden from the death cloud. Once Lionheart's party was further away, the temple island appeared to be nothing more than a sparse rocky sea island.

31. A ROTORCRAFT FROM THE TOWER was the first to site the Caperniean party approaching from beneath the sea.

The following day, Marco and his party arrived at the tower per Lionhearts invitation. Petrov was intrigued with Marco's submersible. It was like an undersea version of a stagecoach. The coach was a streamlined, flat, enclosed structure that was large enough to carry several people. It had a horizontal mast passing through it that pointed in the direction of travel. Four great whites and their riders were harnessed to the central mast, two in the front and two in the rear. After giving Marco's party a tour of the ship, they all departed for the North Dardanelle Reef. Two amphibians from the tower followed Marco's submersible. Marco rode with Lionheart. West and Mullin were in the first amphibian. Peterson, Holsten, Colman (biologist), and Ivanov were in the second. The party was also accompanied by several manned great whites. They made their way into a shallow area, less than seventy feet deep, dominated by colorful reefs all around. Although alien, the site made Lionheart think of times when he was diving in the Caribbean Sea back on Earth. They entered an open area where the reef parted revealing a sandy bottom. Like a king sitting on a throne, a large humanoid fish creature dominated the opposite end. It's left arm extended down, holding what looked like a lighted crystal ball, close to the sandy bottom. Scores of fish were swimming all around. They were two to three feet in length and had large teeth. They made Lionheart think of what a prehistoric piranha fish on Earth might have been like. More appeared as they got closer. Lionheart noticed Marco's submersible and the manned great whites were no longer around. The two amphibians were now alone.

"Steel Fish. Stop. Go no further," Marco said.

"Steel Fish?" Mullin asked.

"Yes. They mostly hunt in warm deep open water near geothermal vents, devouring anything they encounter. In times long past, before the death cloud, the steel fish were known to attack and devour ships. Thankfully for us, the great whites can sense them while they are still at a distance. The steel fish here in what we call Triton's Kings Court, are the only ones we have encountered in shallow waters," Marco said.

"Captain, I'm wondering if coming here to see Triton wasn't a good idea," Mullin said.

"If we were in danger, they would have attacked by now. No one has ever come this close without being attacked before. They appear to be curious," Marco said.

"I don't understand," Lionheart said.

"No one has ever been able to get too close since Triton was first discovered here. The steel fish consumed everyone who tried. I believe he has sensed your presence. He knows you are here. Our legend says, Triton will give the key to Lionheart, and to him, only. That is why we haven't been attacked," Marco said.

Not saying anything, Mullin took a deep swallow. Lionheart stopped and brought the amphibian down on the sandy sea floor, then ordered the second amphibian to do the same.

"If our legend is true, only you can approach Triton," Marco said.

"Well, there's no turning back now," Lionheart said as he took a deep breath and stood up from the pilot seat. Not saying anything, West nodded in agreement.

Minutes later, dressed in a diving suit, Lionheart exited the amphibian alone, keeping a distance. The steel fish began circling all around him. Moving slowly, he walked across the sandy bottom toward Triton. Lionheart had the sensation he was in a grand underwater temple, approaching an oversized statue of a sea god. Triton was big. Even though he was seated and buried almost up to his knees, he was still at least forty feet high. As Lionheart got closer, he could see Triton was holding a small sphere in his right hand. It was similar to the one received from Isis, a crystalline sphere with a multi-colored light pulsing at its center.

32. **AS LIONHEART STEPED AWAY** from the amphibian, he slowly turned and entered the undersea royal court of Triton.

A strange feeling came over Lionheart as he stood before Triton. He felt Triton was trying to speak to him. Lionheart removed his right glove and placed his bare hand on the middle finger of Triton's right hand. For a moment, Lionheart felt he had a connection to Triton's thoughts. He was still alive. At that moment, Lionheart knew Triton was once a human that had also gone through the re-generation process. The other side of re-generation for anyone who has had the experience, is the newly re-generated person is no longer completely human. They are also infused with the properties of a plant that allow for life extension. It was their common plant side that allowed Lionheart and Triton to hear each other's thoughts. Only in Triton's case, someone added several different fish species during the re-generation procedure. The result for him was a half man, half fish hybrid. That was why the steel fish didn't attack Lionheart when he approached. Triton had command over them. There was something else. Lionheart sensed Triton was a direct descendent of one of the towers crew. Lionheart could tell Triton was still very much alive, but without going through the re-generation process again, his plant side had begun to take over. That was a prospect that would face Lionheart at some point in the future. Triton was now in the early stages of merging with the reef. The day was coming when the reef itself would have a collective intelligence, and Triton would be at its center. Lionheart began to see images from Triton's memories. They seemed to be coming from different times and places. Lionheart was becoming confused. Suddenly it all stopped. For the first time he could almost feel Triton was speaking to him directly. *"Take the key now. On this all depends."* Lionheart suddenly had the impression that something pulled Triton's mind away. He was abruptly disturbed by something. But what? Lionheart wondered.

Lionheart pulled his hand away and put his glove back on. He reached into Triton's hand and picked up the sphere. After looking up at Triton one last time, Lionheart started back towards the amphibian. About three quarters of the way, several manned great whites appeared over the area, quickly descending on Lionheart.

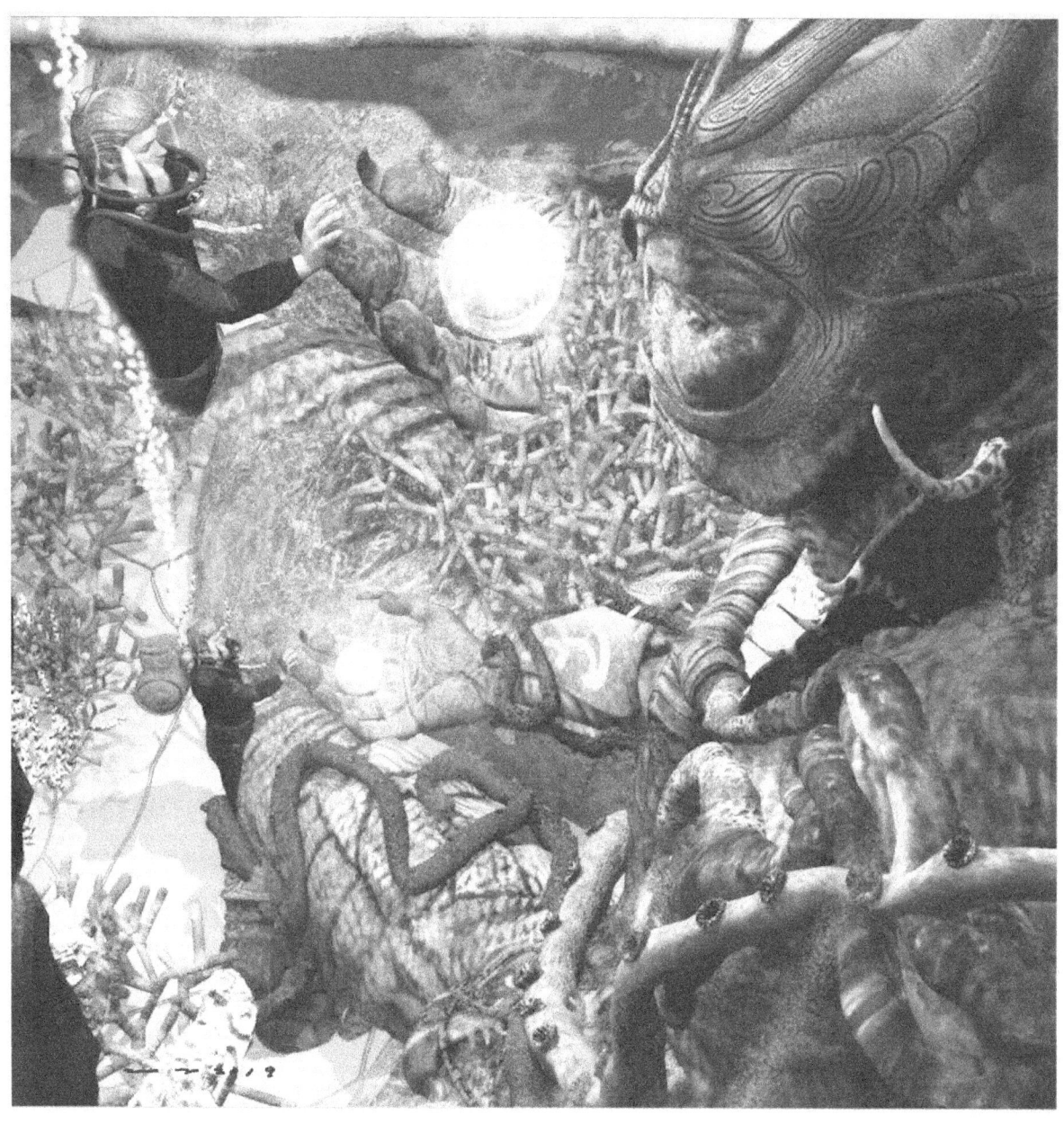

33. **AFTER PLACING HIS HAND** directly on Triton's finger, Lionheart began the hear Triton's thoughts.

Back in the amphibian, everyone was alarmed when they saw the great whites closing in on Lionheart.

"What the hell is going on?" Peterson asked.

"They're going to attack. They're going to attack the Captain. Oh my God," Holsten said.

As they quickly descended, all of the great whites opened their mouths revealing rows of razor-sharp teeth.

"Que Link Co," Marcos said quietly looking up from the amphibian's window.

Just as they were about to attack, two swarms of steel fish closed in on them and in a matter of seconds, the great whites and their Caperniean riders were consumed. Only a cloud of blood and tidbits of bone and flesh remained.

"Magnificent creatures," Ivanov said quietly.

"Que Link Co?" West asked.

"He is the leader of another Caperniean village that broke away from ours many years ago. We understood their desire to go on their own, just as we broke away from the Invergal, but in the years that followed, they began to raid our farms and sea cattle. We fought and won a war against them years ago. We have always known they wanted the key for themselves. They believed possession of the key would put them in a position of power. Every attempt they made has ended like this. I can only assume they are also aware of Lionheart's presence and thought they could recover the key once Lionheart acquired it from Triton," Marco said.

After Lionheart was back on board, they returned to the tower. Marco knew it would be the last time he would see Lionheart. He knew the Captain would now have to seek out the other keys to fulfill his destiny. To the Caperniean, the legend of the key had almost become part of their religion.

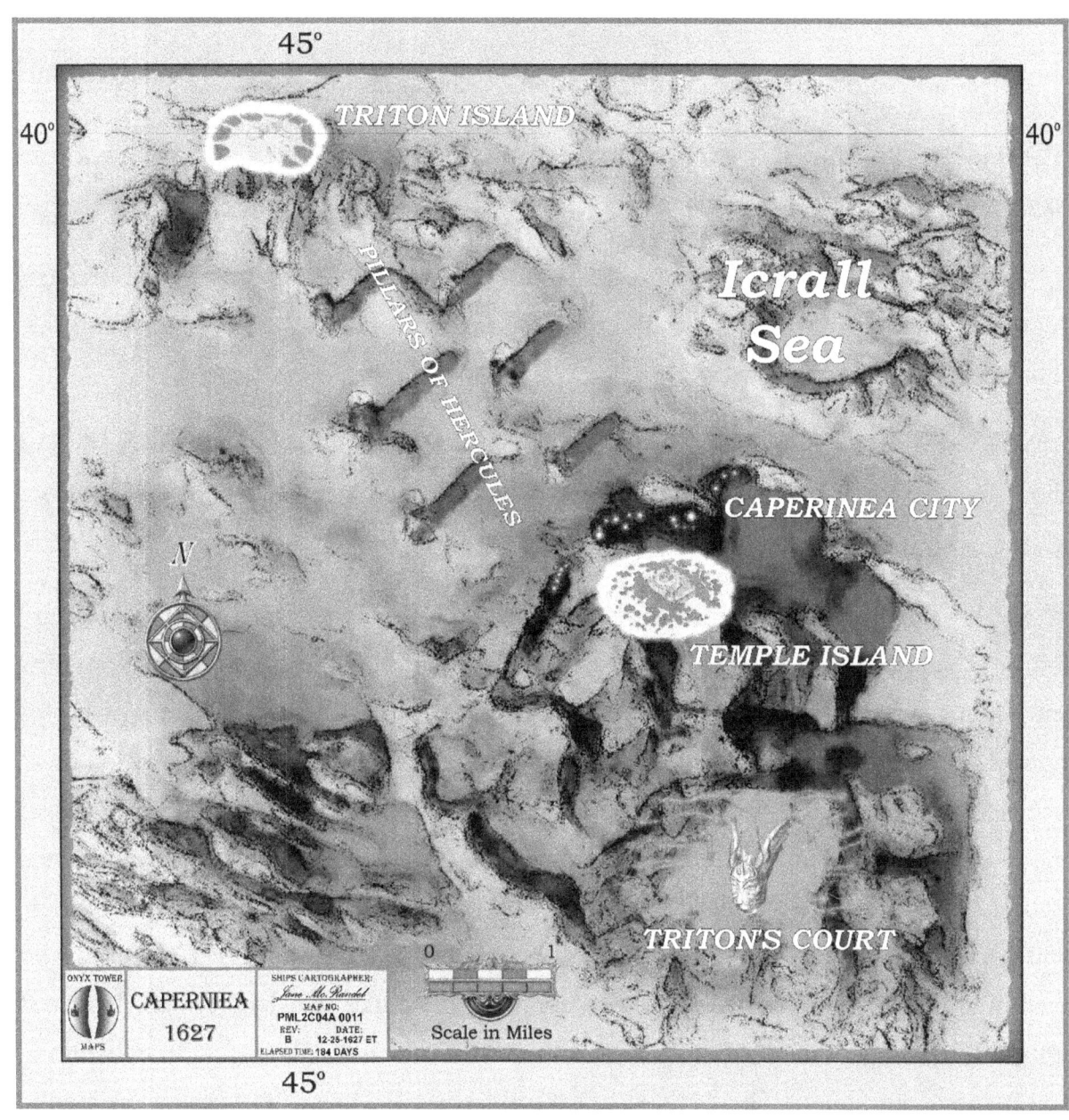

Map labels:

34. **THE UNDERSEA NATION OF CAPERNIEA** in the Earth year of 1627, as rendered by Jane McRandel, ships head cartographer.

"Thank you for all your help. I don't think we could have acquired the second key without you," Lionheart said.

"The second key? You have another one? May I ask where from?" Marco asked.

"We acquired it from the Amadosa," Lionheart said.

"Amadosa, no ship has ever returned from there," Marco quietly said with an expression of fear.

"Based on what we first encountered, I can see why. Some members of our party reported seeing scores of human bones. Do you know the story of Amadosa?" Lionheart asked.

"No one we know of has had direct contact with the Amadosa for centuries. Today, there are only stories and legends. Perhaps Alika can give you the best overview," Marco said.

"As Marco said, there are only stories and legends. Please feel free to add anything I left out," Alika said, looking over at Darius. "Nearly a thousand years ago, the mining settlement of Invergal was founded in the Anaconda Valley. The valley actually got its name because of the deadly stinger snakes that inhabited its jungle. Many settled there because the wealth of minerals in the area outweighed the health risk. There were many deaths in the settlement's early years. Then, the Goddess Belinda came along. Belinda wasn't really a Goddess at all, but rather a human-snake hybrid, and as such, she had mind control over the snakes. The people built a temple in her honor and worshipped her. In exchange for their devotion, the snake attacks stopped. It wasn't long until Belinda decided to expand her power. No longer satisfied with controlling the Invergal settlement, she decided to extend her power over all nearby settlements. At the time, Invergal had a modest security force, which she expanded into a small army. Having control of the snakes, she included them in her arsenal. She used them to invade other settlements before attacking them directly. However, even with all her power, she still met with heavy resistance. The army and her control over snakes weren't enough. Belinda decided to expand her control over insects. To that end, she selected a volunteer from her army and had her re-generate with a dog beetle, "Alika said.

35. **A BRIEF HOSTORY LESSON. Top:** The human-snake hybrid Belinda who once ruled over the Invergal Empire. **Bottom:** After returning to the tower from Triton's court, Alike tells Captain Lionheart and the others of Pangaea's history.

"A dog beetle?" Lionheart asked looking at West and Thornton.

"The dog beetle is a black beetle about the size of a dog, hence the name. They're found mostly in the northern forest, just south of the desert. They are fierce creators. Their armor plating makes them almost impossible to kill and they eat any living flesh. Even the sand fleas are afraid of them," Alika said.

"Excuse me, sand fleas?" Thornton asked.

"They are another fierce predator of the desert. Hopefully you will never encounter them. They have the ability to be completely invisible until attacking with little or no warning. Fortunately, unlike most insects, the dog beetles are few in number," Alika said.

"Please continue," Lionheart said.

"Now, with Belinda's control over snakes and her lieutenant controlling dog beetles, the Invergal army was unstoppable. In time however, Belinda began to question her lieutenant's loyalty and tried to have her killed," Alika said.

"Who was this Lieutenant?" Lionheart asked.

"I think her name was Lance, Lieutenant Lance.", Alika said looking over at Darius for confirmation. "Lance survived the assassination attempt and escaped to the northern desert. It turned out the dog beetle wasn't the only insect Lance had influence over. Once in their proximity, Lance found she could control other deadly insects, and as a result, she had a formidable, non-human army of her own. She went to war with Belinda, but after several battles, the Invergal defeated the insect army. Lance withdrew to avoid capture. The Invergal never found her. Unable to capture Lance, Belinda turned her attention back to the largest colony not under her control, Caperniea. To that end, she decided to create a new hybrid, a large, powerful dragon creature, but that too failed. The creature turned on Belinda and swallowed her whole," Alika said.

36. **LIEUTENANT LANCE,** the human-dog Beatle hybrid who was the first of her kind.

"What happened to Lance?" Lionheart asked.

"After withdrawing from Invergal, Lance fled to a remote location far beyond the reach of Belinda and her army. This is where the story gets interesting. In the years that followed, rumors began to surface about a lone survivor of an expedition that discovered an area ruled by seven beetle-human hybrids. He said the rulers consisted of a mother and six daughters. This story led people to believe Lance laid eggs and those eggs became six daughters or beetle hybrids. This is the only known case where a hybrid of any kind had offspring. According to the survivor, Lance referred to herself and her offspring as the Amadosa and they wanted to start a new race that was half-human.

The stories prompted other expeditions. They found only ruins of what may have been a hive for large insects. They also found the partial remains of Lance. No evidence of any similar hive was discovered in the surrounding lands. However, there's a small group of islands to the northeast, and no expedition has ever returned," Alika said.

"Until now-," Thornton said quietly.

"Many believe any surviving Amadosa would have an even more powerful influence over the local insect life and as such, could easily consume any unwelcome visitors. Since nobody really knows, they later became known as the Amadosa Islands. That was centuries before the death cloud of black oil came to this planet," Alika said.

"The belief that Amadosa is a dangerous place is accurate. Hundreds of beetles attacked our main landing party shortly after we arrived. They stopped only because Isis, a beetle-human hybrid, ordered them to break off the attack. It's doubtful our landing parties would have survived otherwise," Lionheart said.

"It would seem you are temporarily in a very unique position Captain," Marco said.

"What do you mean?" Lionheart asked.

"You are on a place where your coming was foretold by a history you have yet to be a part of. And yet anyone and everyone you encounter who knows of that history will likely help you and allow you to pass to ensure their own history and possibly their very existence, just as Triton and Isis did," Marco said.

"Suppose the time comes when we move on to go back in time. What will happen here?" Thornton asked.

"Things will continue as they would normally with the history of your present time here recorded, completing the legend of your second coming," Marco answered. "You must go to Invergal to acquire the last key. As far as we know, the only remaining one is there. Our historian, Alika has volunteered to help you find it," Marco said.

"Alika's knowledge would be invaluable," West said to Lionheart.

"We would welcome his help. We have a lot to learn about the history of this world," Lionheart said.

Marco wished Lionheart a successful quest and departed. Once his party was off the ship, Lionheart escorted Alika back into the wardroom. A dome projection of Pangaea dominated the large round electronic 3d image table. Alika was amazed at the sight of it. Long ago when Caperniea was still on land, electricity was used, but it was centuries ago. For many Caperniean generations, the use of electricity was known only by ancestral stories.

"I'm amazed by your tower, Captain. There were many stories, but I never imagined what it might actually be like. I expected it to be more like a mythical flying castle made of stone," Alika said.

"We have a lot to learn from each other. I hope you can tell us the best place to find the key when we reach Invergal," Lionheart said.

"I can't say for sure, but my best guess would be somewhere in the Invergal capital city. It was one of the earliest and largest of recent human settlements," Alika said.

"Recent human settlements?" West asked.

"Yes, that is the term used for human settlements from approximately a thousand years ago. The Invergal Empire was the greatest and the largest. As I said, I believe there is a very good chance the key you are looking for will be somewhere in their capital city, in the Temple of the Snake, or at least what is left of it," Alika said.

"Where exactly is this capital city?" Lionheart asked.

Alika stepped closer to the luminous dome map and studied it carefully. "The nearest coastline directly west of here is called Baku valley at the mouth of the Antilles river," Alika said pointing. "If you follow the river, it leads down through the Kiber Pass in the Jenolan Mountains to Avalon Lake at the northern end of the Gobin Desert. The Caucasus Mountains lay at the southern end of Gobin Desert. The Anaconda Valley, home of the Invergal Empire, is on the southern side of the Caucasus Mountains," Alika said.

"How much do you know about the Invergal Empire?" Holsten asked.

"I know only of the stories from our history. After what was later described as the dragon war, when Belinda was swallowed up, we had no direct contact with the Invergal. As the years passed, many among us became curious about the Invergal. With Belinda gone, some believed her empire had been consumed by snakes. I think our leaders at the time were more worried then curious. About this time, a small airship was constructed to carry an expedition team hundreds of miles across the desert to the Caucasus Mountains. They were to quietly reach the outer border of the Empire and return in one month's time. When the time for their return came and went, we feared the worst. Then, six months later the only survivor was rescued in the desert, a hundred miles away from Lake Avalon. Thru him, we learned of what happened after Belinda was gone," Alika said. At that point everyone was quiet and waited for him to continue. "We learned after Belinda was gone, her centurions took over," Alika said.

"Her Centurions?" Lionheart asked.

"They were Belinda's bodyguards. She had them created shortly after she came to power," Alika said.

"Created?" Thornton asked.

"She had them altered to become superior physically, to have their strength and endurance greatly increased. There was only a small number of them, but it was said they were impossible to kill. Their skin was said to be like the bark of a tree," Alika said.

Not saying anything, West looked at Lionheart.

"Was there anything else?" Lionheart asked.

"Only that the centurions were losing control of the Empire. They were known to be very cruel. Also, after Belinda was gone, the snakes returned. Many people were killed. At the time of our expedition, several groups were fleeing the Empire. It was one such group that helped the only survivor to escape. He said a golden temple had been built and the centurions fiercely guarded it. I believe the key you seek is there, in the Temple of the Snake," Alika said.

"All right. We will depart for the Caucasus Mountains tomorrow morning after Petrov has completed his recalibration of the ships internal drive," Lionheart commanded.

THE PORTAL

Having the ability to transcend time and space at will, Ivanov's Guardian had amassed great power over the centuries. Yet in spite of his power, he knew his life was locked in a long pattern of events that there was no escape from. His entire future was part of his memory, and there was nothing he could do to change it. He knew when he reached the end of his life, it would start all over again, and it would all unfold just as it did before. As he continued down his life's path knowing everything that was going to happen, there was a deep madness in the back of his mind that longed for death.

When he was a young boy in China, the hillside palace he lived in was surrounded by beautiful gardens. He learned, for the plants to reach their full potential, they had to be pruned back occasionally. The Guardian felt the same applied to humanity. He was very creative and soon learned there were many ways to accomplished his goals. The one he enjoyed the most was to sow chaos. Unleashing horror on the unsuspecting was so pleasurable it made him giddy.

The year was 2183. Much of the planet Venus had been terraformed to become Earth like. Seas and oceans had formed across the planet by this time. A protective transparent bubble began to form in the warm, pea green undersea waters not far from the equator. When the bubble was large enough the Guardian appeared in it. Using the powers at his command he opened an underwater doorway to the seas of Pangaea from the year 1627.

Somewhere in the dark waters not far from the Caperniea, a school of steel fish were looking for their next meal. They sensed movement in the dark waters ahead. As they swam towards it a light appeared behind them. A strong current began to pull them backwards toward the light. It was like a crackling ball of lightning and a whirlpool was forming around it. For the first time the steel fish were feeling a new sensation, fear. They panicked and swam out in all directions as fast as they could, but it was to no avail, the current was pulling them in.

37. **THE FRIGHTENED SCHOOL OF STEEL FISH,** were unable to escape from the underwater vortex that was pulling them in.

As the bright water all around them began to flash and pulse, they felt the water was becoming much warner and the sunlight was different. They were being pulled through a doorway that led to a planet one thousand lightyears away and 556 years in the future. The flashing light faded, revealing a clear, pea-green sea all around them. They were now in one of many newly formed oceans on a terraformed Venus. As the panic wore off, the steel fish formed back into a school and continued to hunt for prey. They soon detected something in the water not far away. It was a small sailboat moving across the gentle surface above. Once again, they focused only on their hunger and hostility. It was feeding time. Within minutes, they devoured the boat and the one man sailing it. In a short while, all that remained were small fragments of the boat's wooden hull, floating on the surface. It's one occupant was completely devoured. The steel fish even consumed the bone fragments.

From a safe underwater vantage point, the Guardian quietly laughed to himself as the terrifying scene played out. He felt it was appropriate to pull the school of steel fish from the time and place when he first saw them devour the manned great whites that tried to attack Lionheart.

One of the ways he enjoyed sowing chaos was by moving samples of life forms from one world to the next, from one time to another, just to see what would happen. Here on Venus, the year was 2183. He was amused by the terror and havoc the steel fish would bring to an unsuspecting population of newcomers from Earth. The Guardian also wondered how they would fair against some of the other dangerous life forms brought in from other worlds. It made him happy to know that the investigation of the steel fish origin in a newly formed ocean would drive the investigators mad with speculation.

38. **THE GUARDIAN** introduces Pangaean steel fish to the warm waters of Venus.

INVERGAL

At first light, the Onyx Tower rose up out of the sea and departed from Caperniea. Lionheart wasn't sure why, but he wanted to take his time getting to Invergal. A voice in his head told him to take it slowly. After reaching an altitude of only five thousand feet, he had the tower fly southwest following the route Alika pointed out earlier. As they reached the coastline, Lionheart had the tower slow down. Moving at the approximate speed of an airship gave everyone time to observe the land in greater detail. As they passed over the Baku Valley, Lionheart was reminded of the ruins they visited on Pangaea's sister planet, Torlon. The entire capital city of Caperniea lay in ruin below. Alika had no emotion as they flew over the city of his ancestors. He knew it would take several generations before it was restored to its former glory.

Following the Antilles River, the Onyx Tower continued on through the Kiber pass and onto the Gobin Desert. Moving south of the Jenolan Mountains they came upon Avalon Lake. The deep blue lake stood out against the flat barren surrounding desert. The appearance of the desert was deceiving. It was actually at a slightly higher elevation then the Kiber Pass. The Gobin desert seemed like another world. The featureless, flat land seemed endless in all directions. Thornton wondered how the early Capernieans managed to cross it.

"Alika, how did your people manage to cross this desert? There is no sign of water for miles in any direction," Thornton asked.

"There is water. South of Avalon Lake, the Antilles River continues underground. You wouldn't know it unless you knew what to look for," Alika said as he stepped closer to Thornton. "Look down there. Do you see that small fissure?" He pointed at what looked like a long crack on the desert floor. "The river runs shallow there. If you dig you won't have to go very deep to find it," Alika said.

It began to get darker as the sun set. The sky became a dome of brilliant stars and the glowing clouds of the Plutarius nebula. As it got darker, the desert floor turned green under the nebula's light. Ground features were almost visible. Lionheart returned to his cabin to rest. For no reason, he began to think of Argosh in his dreams. The next morning, Lionheart looked out at the early sunrise. The desert itself appeared flat and lifeless. Occasionally, he heard the faint sounds of wind rushing past his window as the tower passed through the up and down drafts over the desert below. He looked at his timepiece. In a few hours, they would reach an area in the central Gobin desert called the South Dardanelles. They consisted of a grand collection of individual plateaus, grouped together forming an archipelago in the middle of the vast surrounding desert. There was a knock at his door.

"Come in."

"Good morning Captain," West responded entering the cabin.

"Good morning West. I had another one of my dreams last night," Lionheart said.

"Was Argosh in it?"

"Yes. I don't understand why these dreams keep reoccurring. It's almost as though Argosh is actually a ghost who haunts my dreams."

"What was your dream about this time?" West asked.

"It started out the same. I was back in the garden at my Aunt Fern's house in London. As I got to the lockbox there were now two keys in it. They were in the top and middle locks. I looked into the bottom and last keyhole of the lock box. This time a green light was shining out of it. Looking closer, I saw what appeared to be a dense jungle. The next thing I knew we were in it, walking through the ruins of a city. We were in danger, but not from any animals in the jungle. Something else was there. There was a temple, and standing on the steps outside the entrance, someone, pointed for us to go inside. I think it was Argosh, but I couldn't see him clearly. When we reached the top of the steps, he was gone. There was a long corridor inside and at the end of it was an open area with a pedestal at its center. There was a white ball of light hovering above it. As I stepped closer, the light flashed and the next thing I knew I was in a dense dust storm somewhere in the desert. I strained to see around me, but the dust was so thick it was almost impossible. Then, there was a brief lull in the storm, and I could see the shadow outlines of tall desert monoliths all around. A second later, the storm increased. I woke up gasping for air as though I had inhaled dust," Lionheart said.

39. **TWO KEYS NOW OCCUPY THE LOCKBOX** as Lionheart has another reoccurring dream. As Lionheart looks closer at the bottom keyhole he sees visions of a jungle only to find himself is a dust storm.

West was silent for a moment as she processed what Lionheart said. Her only response was "Interesting. Captain, I'm curious as to why you chose to fly at our current rate of speed. The tower is scarcely traveling at eighty miles an hour. At this rate, we will not reach Invergal until mid-morning tomorrow," West asked.

"I can't give any logical answer. Something tells me to take my time reaching Invergal. I have this feeling-", Lionheart said, pausing for a moment, "We should reach the South Dardanelles in a few hours."

"They are one of the more unusual areas on this planet," West said.

"When we reach them have Quinn adjust our altitude to fly just above them, and set the towers sensors to full," Lionheart ordered.

"Are you looking for something?" West asked.

"I don't know. I just can't stop thinking about them for some reason. I have a strong sense there is something out here," Lionheart said, leaning back in his chair.

Hours later, the Onyx Tower reached the Dardanelles. The tower increased altitude to fly above them. It was a strange place. The thousands of monoliths were arranged in such a way that made the land below appear as though the planet was breaking up. Beyond the stunning vistas, the flight over the Dardanelles was uneventful. Moving further south, the tower was once again over flat, endless desert. At the first light of next morning, a mountain range appeared in the horizon ahead. It meant they were finally reaching the southern end of the Gobin Desert.

40. IN ROUTE TO INVERGAL, The Onyx Tower passes over the South Dardanelles.

The com sounded in Lionheart's cabin.

"Captain here," Lionheart said.

"Captain, you wanted to be informed when we reached the Caucasus Mountains. We should arrive at Invergal in about an hour," Thornton said.

"Ok, very good Thornton. Captain out," Lionheart said.

What seemed like endless desert finally changed as the tower began to pass over the Caucasus range. Even though the mission was far from over, Lionheart felt the change in scenery would be good for the crew. The mountains below were dry and rugged at first, but as they got further south, the dryness gave way to higher humidity and the rugged mountainside disappeared under thick jungle vegetation. The area reminded Lionheart when they first arrived on Pangaea. The Anaconda Valley was just over the next ridge. When they saw the remains of the city, it was what Lionheart expected it to be. It mostly resembled what one might expect to find in the jungles of Central America back on Earth. Lionheart assumed it would be uninhabited. Even though he knew the area had rich mineral deposits, he still wondered why anyone would settle in a snake infested, steamy jungle. Then he saw the golden domes. They were everywhere. He heard stories of vast gold deposits in the surrounding area.

"All Stop. Mr. Quinn, hold our current position," Lionheart commanded.

"Aye Sir, holding position," Quinn responded.

Five hundred feet below the tower was the temple of the snake, Belinda's temple. It was one of the larger buildings of the inner city, characterized by large, opposite facing, headless statues of Belinda on top of it. Lionheart wondered if Belinda's head had to be removed just as Medusa's was.

"That's it, the temple of the snake. That is where we need to go," Lionheart said.

"Is that what you saw in your dream?" West asked quietly.

"No, I only have a strong sense what we are looking for is somewhere down there inside that temple. We will send two landing parties. West, you, Dr. Alliot, Mullin and I will take the first rotorcraft. Peterson, Moss and a Hanson unit will take the second. Mr. Thornton, you have the com."

"Captain, why Alliot?" West asked.

"Were going into an old temple. My guess is it has been there for at least 800 years. If there are any images, writing or symbols on its walls, who better to have around than an expert in ancient languages. Mr. Quinn, scan the area below in infrared. I would like to know if there is any dangerous animal life close by," Lionheart said.

"Aye Sir, scanning now."

"Captain, no snakes or other animal life detected, however there are several trees among the dead wood below that have higher temperature readings. I put the image up on the main view," Quinn said.

"West?" Lionheart asked.

"Unknown Captain, the increase in temperature of a tree in decomposition is not unusual, but I can't explain the variance in temperature, especially when the hot trees are not in direct contact with the cold dead trees surrounding them," West said looking at the images.

"Do you mean like mulch becomes steamy when mixed?" Lionheart asked.

"Yes. Decomposing plants often heat up when only when they are compressed together in a pile," West said.

"Well, it's probably nothing we should be concerned with. Let's get to the launch bay. Mr. Thornton hold our current position above the city. You have the com," Lionheart said.

41. **THE ONYX TOWER** arrives at the Invergal capital.

The First rotorcraft lifted off from the tower and landed in a clearing near the base of the temple. After dropping off the Hanson unit, Peterson and Moss lifted off in the and began circling, watching the as the second rotorcraft with Lionheart's party landed near the base of the temple.

"This must have been a great city once," Lionheart said as he started up the steep, wide temple steps. The temple entrance was high above them. He estimated approximately 250 feet [76 meters] to reach it. As they ascended, Lionheart kept looking out at the surrounding city. He wondered what the day of carnage must have been like when the black oil death cloud first descended on an unsuspecting population. Looking down at the steps, he also wondered how many seasons of rain it took to wash away the blood and bone remains.

West detected sounds of movement coming from the area of dead trees surrounding the temple base. The sound was so faint, only she could hear it. To the normal ear, any sound of wind blowing through the ruins of a dead city were drowned out by the deep steady pulse coming from the Onyx Tower as it hovered high above. Looking back at the dead forest below, West changed her vision to infrared to detect possible predators. There was no sign of any animal. As before, West saw only dead plants with a few warmer ones mixed in, but something was not right. West ran an analysis to make a further determination.

They were about halfway up. West stopped. She realized what it was. The first image taken from the tower above did not match what she observed from the steps. The hot plants had moved.

"West, what is it?" Lionheart asked.

"Captain, some of the plants below are moving," West said.

Turning around, Lionheart and West could see some of the dead trees had closed off the path at the base of the steps. West instructed the hanson unit below to turn, aim its cannons at the approaching trees and open fire.

42. **WEST INSTRUCTED THE HANSON UNIT** to turn, aim and open fire in the trees approaching the base of the pyramid. After the first burst of fire, the Hanson stepped up behind Lionheart's party to block the trees path.

After stopping for a moment, the undamaged trees moved forward and started moving up the steps. They didn't look like trees in the traditional sense. They were more like crawling vines, walking on all fours like a dog. This impression was supported because each of them had two forward horizontal branches, one on top of the other and each branch had a row of sharp teeth on the side facing the opposite branch. The approaching trees were large, about the approximate size of a fully-grown elephant.

"West, Mullin!" Lionheart yelled as he raised his gun and fired a lightning bolt down at the approaching trees. West and Mullin did the same. West nodded at the Hanson to continue firing it's cannons. The lightning fire only slowed the trees. Lionheart knew they would be upon his party in a few minutes. Some of the trees were beginning to smoke. The ones in the front started to catch fire and crumble. As they did, more trees approaching from behind brushed them aside and continued climbing. Lionheart knew their lightning weapons would soon lose their charge.

"Dammit. Where the hell is Peterson?" Lionheart shouted.

"I'm right here Captain," Peterson said as he flew up from the backside of the temple. Passing over the landing party, Peterson began firing on the trees. The trees below exploded into fragments of burning wood. Doctor Alliot cried out in pain. Lionheart turned around just in time to see him snatched up by one of three trees that came out of the temples entrance above. Lionheart and Mullin turned, firing at tree's legs. Releasing Alliot, the tree stumbled and tumbled down the steps into the burning pile below. Two more trees came out of the temple above and started to close in on Lionheart's party. Lionheart, West and Mullin fired a short burst from their guns. That was all they had left. As they started to run back down the steps, Peterson flew in overhead and opened fire. The remaining trees caught fire and exploded. Everyone dodged the flying pieces of burning wood as the trees tumbled down the temple's steps. The attack was over, at least for now. West made her way over to Alliot. Getting down on one knee West turned him over.

"He's dead Pete," West said quietly as Lionheart approached.

43. LIONHEART'S LANDING PARTY came under attack as they made their way up to the temple.

"Captain, Thornton here."

"Go ahead Thornton," Lionheart said.

"Captain, ships sensors indicate the few remaining hot trees are moving away from your position. I've dispatched another rotorcraft in case they return," Thornton said.

"Very good Thornton, Lionheart out." Looking up, Lionheart could see the other rotorcraft as it left the tower. During the firefight, Lionheart knew Thornton could not fire the towers powerful weapons without destroying the entire area. He ordered the flying rotorcraft to defend the temple entrance once the landing party went inside. Lionheart was not surprised to see the inner temple hallway was much like the one of his earlier dream. It led to an open area with a block pedestal in the center, surrounded by a pool of water. There were columns surrounding the area with barren trees all around.

Using infrared vision, West looked all around and saw only one hot tree. Passing the information on to the Hansen, it raised its cannons and waited for the command to fire. This tree was different from the ones below. It was more upright. It gave West the impression of being more humanoid in appearance. West became curious. She didn't want the tree destroyed until having a chance to study it further. Lionheart and West stepped out on the narrow walkway that led to the central pillar.

"Well, the energy stone was here at one time," Lionheart said as he looked at the round indentation on the pedestal's top.

"So, the great tower captain arrives to find another key to the past," The hot tree said in a deep, gravelly voice.

Somewhat startled, Lionheart and Mullin turned to look up at the speaking tree. This one had a mouth on its trunk. The Hanson stood ready to fire its weapon as it waited for the command to do so. West motioned at it to stand by.

"Who are you?" Lionheart asked.

"As a man I was Kalladon, First Captain of the Temple Centurions. Now I am only part of the living dead garden that surrounds what is left of Belinda's Temple," Kalladon answered.

"I don't understand. What were the centurions and how did you come to be like this?" Lionheart asked even though he already knew the answer to the last part of his question. It was obvious Kalladon had gone through the regeneration process. However, in order to maintain its effect, one had to repeat the process approximately once every 50 Earth years. If one failed to do so, he would become more and more physically plant like as the years passed. Looking at the tree, West also knew why, but said nothing.

"Many centuries ago, this was once a great empire that was ruled and protected by the Goddess Belinda. We loved and worshiped her. Shortly after she came to rule over Invergal, Belinda offered a small, select, group of solders the opportunity to become centurions, protectors of her temple. In exchange for our services, we received the blessing of immortality. Each one of us went through a ceremony that marked our rebirth into new, stronger bodies. In the early years the centurions not only protected the temple, but we were also a small elite fighting force. Every few decades we repeated the same ceremony that renewed our bodies so we could continue as centurions, but as time passed, the ceremonies grew further and further apart and eventually stopped altogether. In the years that followed we started changing. Our bodies started becoming more plant like. It was after the battle of the Dragon that the ceremonies stopped completely. All of the centurions evolved into living trees. It has been a horrible curse we can't escape from," Kalladon said.

"So, the trees that attack us, they were once centurions?" Lionheart asked.

"No. They were hybrid solders that were mixed with a land animal when they went through the body regeneration ceremony. That is why they are much larger and walk on four legs," Kalladon said.

"Why did they attack us?" Lionheart asked.

"The legend of the Onyx Tower is well known. According to it, the tower would arrive at a distant time in the future before traveling back to the beginning, back to start the next human civilization on Pangaea. The hybrid solders attacked you because they decided it was their best chance to alter the timeline of history. By killing the tower's Captain, they believe their history would change. They believed it would be better to face the possibility of never being born then to endure the living curse of their existence," Kalladon said.

"Kalladon, what about you? Where do you stand with all this?" Lionheart asked.

"I agree with my fellow centurions completely, but I don't think killing you is necessary. All I need to do is prevent you from going back in time. You can't unlock that door without the keys," Kalladon said.

"So, there was an energy stone here at one time?" Lionheart asked, looking at the indentation on the pillar.

"Yes, it was here, but it's gone now to a place far away."

"Where?" Lionheart asked.

"Since you will probably all be killed anyway; I might as well tell you. It is on an island in the sea of the far north. It is on the island of Amadosa. I arranged to have it delivered there years ago. I knew once there; it could never be retrieved. You see no one has ever returned from Amadosa, no one," Kalladon said.

"Well, we have to try.", Lionheart said with a faint smile. Lionheart had the sense Kalladon, and the other centurions had a lived a somewhat primitive existence, equivalent to the early nations of central and south America. Kalladon also didn't know that the energy stone at Amadosa had already been acquired. "There was a third key out there somewhere, but where?" Lionheart thought to himself.

44. LIONHEART'S PARTY meets with Kalladon, first captain of the Invergal temple centurions.

"Good luck," was the last thing Kalladon said before Lionheart's party departed. Lionheart also wondered how the centurions survived the black oil death cloud. West told him the temple had a field sphere, similar to those found at Crystor's Gate and Caperniea. No one (except West) noticed the temperature change when Lionheart's party first arrived because they were fighting for their lives.

After the landing party returned to the tower, Lionheart met with West and Thornton in the wardroom.

"Have you completed your analysis of the South Dardanelles?" Lionheart asked.

"I have Captain. Scans of the immediate area surrounding the tower revealed nothing out of the ordinary. However, one of the drones, sent to the very southern edge of the Dardanelles, detected something interesting. There is a small monolith island group that have several separate areas having the exact same temperature. The areas were too small to be detected earlier," West said, placing an infrared image down in front of Lionheart.

"+72°F [+22.2°C]?" Lionheart asked.

"Precisely, this would seem to indicate there may be several field generators, similar to the one found at Crystor's Gate, and if so, there is the possibility the area may be inhabited," West said.

"Very good West. Mr. Thornton set course for the southern edge of the South Dardanelle chain. Ahead, steady as she goes. Set speed to arrive tomorrow morning," Lionheart ordered.

"Aye Caption," Thornton responded as he left the wardroom.

"Tomorrow morning?" West asked.

"Yes, as crazy as it sounds, I want to have a sleep period before we get there," Lionheart said.

"You are hoping Argosh will come to you in your dreams?" West said.

"Yes. I'm hoping Argosh will provide clues as to what lies ahead, although, between you and me, I haven't ruled out the possibility that he could be a product of my overactive imagination."

45. **THE AREA OF INTEREST** is displayed on the wardroom's luminary table as West reveals the place where a small group of monolith islands have the exact same temperature.

NORCONIEA

Alone in his cabin, Captain Lionheart looked out of his window. The night desert began to turn from brown to red orange under the bright light of Torlon rising in the east. It was brighter than the light of a full moon on Earth. Resting on his couch, Lionheart dozed off. As before, he found himself back in Kensington Park, London, standing near the back door of his Aunt Ferns. Everything looked the same at first. As he stepped closer to the back door, the two keys that were once in the three-lock box were now in his hand. Looking back at the lock box, a red-orange light began to shine out of the bottom keyhole. He got down to get a closer look. The next thing Lionheart knew, he was in a large network of underground caves. Everything was bathed in the red-orange glow of torches and lanterns all around. Lionheart was immediately reminded of the underground mining city of Antopav in western Siberia. Only this cavern was different. There were no people, only machines. The scene changed. Lionheart was standing on the bright sunny beach of a tall rocky island, only there was no surrounding water. The land beyond the rolling sand dunes that surrounded the island was only flat, parched, desert, extending to the distant horizon in all directions. Feeling the presence of someone standing behind him, Lionheart quickly turned around. It was Argosh. Before Lionheart could respond he said, "Only that which crawls through the sand, can take you to the hidden land." The scene changed again, and Lionheart was standing out on the dunes, away from the island. Something was moving in the sand not far away. It was like a small whale, moving just below the surface. It turned toward Lionheart. He tried to run, but the deep sand made it almost impossible for him to move his feet. The harder he tried, the harder it was to move. The rocky island was too far away to reach in time. As the rolling mound of sand got closer, Lionheart could hear the sound of a deep pulsing machine. When it was almost upon Lionheart, a giant worm-like machine came up out of the sand. Its sharp nose opened up as to swallow Lionheart. Flinching to defend himself, he woke up. It was morning. Looking out the window, he could see the clear shadow of the tower cast on the desert below. He was certain his dream was related to a future event. The question was when. He didn't have to wait long. The tone of his com sounded. "Yes," he responded.

46. **LIONHEART HAS ANOTHER DREAM.** This time the two keys that were once in the lock box, were now in his hand. Argosh appeared saying "Only that which crawls through the sand, can take you to the hidden land."

"Captain," Thornton said.

"Go ahead Thornton."

"Captain, there are some unusual land features up ahead. We are approaching southern edge of the South Dardanelle chain. They look like the islands, West showed us in the wardroom sir," Thornton said.

"I'm on my way," Lionheart responded.

Minutes later, Lionheart stepped on to the bridge. A grand column of rock appeared in the distant horizon. Like a steep volcanic island high above the surrounding ocean, the monolith rose several thousand feet above the desert. It was flanked by several smaller outcrop islands to the southwest. This was the southern end of the Dardanelle mountain chain.

"What do you make of it, Thornton," Lionheart asked, looking at the outcrop ahead.

"I'm reminded of similar formations in the southwest United States," Thornton said.

"Yes, but this looks to be much larger. I've only seen features like these in low gravity worlds. The way the islands are arranged reminds me of the Florida Keys. Get Alika on the bridge. I'm wonder if he knows anything," Lionheart said. At that moment Alika and Connors stepped on the bridge.

"Norco," Alika said quietly.

"Excuse me?" Lionheart asked.

"We are coming up on the islands of Norco. They were first discovered by my ancestors when they fled from the Invergal Empire. The islands were said to be rich in minerals, but our people didn't stay long. They wanted to get further away from the Invergal and at the time there wasn't enough water to sustain them," Alika said as the tower passed over one of the smaller outer islands. As they got closer, the desert floor began to change. The flat hard ground gave way to large rolling sand dunes. In a way,

114

they added to the illusion of the ocean island effect. Many of the larger islands had green vegetation on top. Lionheart wondered if anyone tried to settle here.

"Alika, do you know if anyone ever made it to the top of that mountain?" Lionheart asked, pointing to the dominant, cloud covered island.

"As far as I know it was never attempted. The walls were too steep," Alika said.

"Mr. Quinn," Lionheart said.

"Aye sir," Quinn responded.

"Take us up over the mountain ahead."

"Aye sir."

The Onyx tower began to gain altitude as it approached Norco's main island. Moments later, the tower reached twelve thousand feet. The mountain top was less than two thousand feet below. The mountain itself was actually a steep, ten-thousand-foot wall, encircling a dark, shadowed valley interior. The valley floor was clearly visible. It was covered by a reflective crystalline surface. From a distance, it had the appearance of a lake reflecting the overhead sky.

"All stop," Lionheart commanded.

"The floor of that valley is so deep. I bet it's never in full sunlight," Thornton said.

"Fascinating, it reminds me of the entrance to Crystor," Connors said.

"I had the same impression. Mr. Quinn, take us down slowly. I want to get a closer look," Lionheart commanded.

"Aye sir," Quinn responded.

47. HAVING ARRIVED AT THE ISLAND GROUP, The Onyx Tower slowly ascends to the top of the main island.

The tower started a slow decent. It wasn't long until the tower entered the valley's shadow. Down in engineering, where the energy keys were stored, the keys themselves were starting to glow brighter. No one noticed it at first. Engineer Petrov had his back to the keys while making a routine systems check when he noticed his shadow was cast in the control panel in front of him.

As the tower descended deeper into the valley shadows the crystal floor slowly began to shine by its own light, forming a soft glow at first.

"Captain, ships sensors are detecting a faint energy surge," West said.

"Where is the source?" Lionheart asked.

"It is coming from the valley floor directly beneath us," At that moment, sparks of flashing lights began on the valley floor.

Down in engineering, Petrov realized a bright light was behind him. The keys began to crackle with energy. Somewhat startled, he slowly turned around. Small bolts of lightning began to discharge from the key containers. Walking in, McDoogen jumped across the chamber and hit the master alarm before landing on the floor. Petrov and Jacobs rushed over, picked McDoogen up and pulled him out of the chamber, sealing the doorway behind them.

"Petrov, this is Lionheart. What is going on down there?"

"Captain, the energy keys have become active and are becoming unstable. I don't know if they can be contained," Petrov said.

The valley floor was becoming brighter, and bolts of lightning began to discharge, with some of them striking the tower. When they did, lightning bolts emanated from the keys in engineering, striking the chamber walls all around.

"Captain, we have to get out of here. The energy field forming below is directly linked to the keys in engineering," West said.

48. **AS THE ONYX TOWER DECENDED** the energy keys in engineering started to become dangerously unstable. The once quiet valley floor began to pulse with energy as lightning bolts from it began to strike the tower.

"Mr. Quinn, get us out of here! West raise the shields," Lionheart shouted.

"Ayer sir," Quinn answered. The tower started to ascend.

"Shields are not responding Captain. The system has sustained internal damage from the energy keys," West responded.

As the tower got higher, the energy field below started to diminish. Petrov and his crew did their best to protect engineering, but the damage was considerable. Petrov knew he was fighting a losing battle when suddenly, lightning from the energy keys faded away and stopped. The tower came up from the center valley and passed over the mountain rim. Looking back Lionheart could see that the valley floor had become calm again. The lightning had stopped, and the keys in engineering became quiet as before.

"What was that?" Thornton asked.

"I'm not sure. It felt like the proximity of the tower over the valley floor had the effect of a static discharge, or it might possibly have been some sort of defense system. West?" Lionheart asked.

"This reaction confirms the energy field has a direct correlation to the energy keys on board. I also detected a faint, unusual pattern of energy flow. It acted in the form a circular pattern. I will do a further analysis," West said.

"What now captain?" Thornton asked.

"I'm curious about the surrounding area. Mr. Quinn," Lionheart said.

"Aye sir," Quinn responded.

"Take us back down to the base of the mountain. Set altitude at 2000 feet but adjust altitude as required for every island we pass over. Put us on a slow circular course that takes us around the mountain on a gradual spiral outward, moving further away with each orbit," Lionheart commanded.

"Aye sir."

"I'm curious captain. What do you hope to find?" Connors asked.

"I can't say for sure, but I feel there is a lot more to all the surrounding desert islands then meets the eye," Lionheart said.

Once down near the base of the mountain, the Onyx Tower began slowly moving outward with each pass, carefully surveying every island it flew over.

"It is strange how the land surrounding the mountain and its rocky islands have rolling sand dunes, unlike the hard-baked floor of the desert beyond," Thornton said.

"Any thoughts as to why that is Mrs. Bascom?" Lionheart asked the ships head geologist.

"Not that I can discern without collecting samples. I have seen examples of soil changes around outcrops in deserts before, but nothing this extreme. It's is almost as though-," Bascom stopped.

"Almost as though what?" Lionheart asked.

"Sir, it's almost as though it was somehow repeatedly being plowed up by something over a period of many years. I know that doesn't make any sense," Bascom said.

"Alika said Norco was rich in minerals. It's possible the Invergal might have had surface mining operations here at one time, hundreds of years ago," West said.

"If they did, they would have been killed off by the death cloud," Thornton said.

"West, have you detected anything unusual on the islands we've passed over?" Lionheart asked.

"Many of the Islands surveyed so far seem to be contrary to Alika's previous description," West said.

"What do you mean?" Lionheart asked.

"Alika said the area had insufficient water to support the Caperniean settlers, yet on most of the larger islands, small lagoons with surrounding vegetation have been detected. It would seem tops of this mountain group are actually covered by an oasis, making them ideal for possible settlement. The largest one detected so far is just ahead. There is something else. As I said before, we detected several oases with the exact same temperature, +72°F [+22.2°C]. All stop," West commanded.

The tower stopped above one of the green islands. West adjusted the bridge viewing screen to focus on an area below.

"West, what is it?" Lionheart asked.

"Captain, look there," West said, pointing.

"It's a sphere with three columns, like the one at Crystor's Gate," Connors said.

"Yes doctor. It would seem there are several areas below that may have gone undetected by the death cloud and as such, may still be inhabited. It is also possible when the Invergal came here, they might have been around long enough to discover a subterranean water source, and develop it, at least to some extent. Any thoughts captain?" West asked.

Lionheart sat quietly for a moment. "Mr. Quinn, move the tower out approximately five miles beyond the dune perimeter and set us down. I want to have a closer look at this island."

"Captain, Petrov here."

"Go ahead Petrov," Lionheart said.

"Captain, we have a problem. We have to land as soon as possible. The discharge from the keys has damaged our energy fuses. Only thirty percent are still operating, and they won't last long," Petrov said.

49. AS THE ONYX TOWER PASSED over one of the larger islands, the sphere supported by columns was clearly visible. Lionheart and the others knew the force fields covering the islands might have also concealed a living population from the death cloud.

"Very well Petrov. Mr. Quinn, set us down as soon as you can," Lionheart commanded.

"Aye Captain," Quinn responded.

"Mr. Thornton, you have the com. I'll be down in engineering," Lionheart said as he left the bridge.

The tower landed. Just after touching down, Petrov started to shut down the internal drive but stopped when he noticed the tower suddenly listing to one side. When the tower started sinking into the sand he increased the internal drive power and helmsman Quinn brought the tower back up in the air.

"Petrov, what is happening down there?" Lionheart asked.

"After making contact with the ground we started sinking. It is not safe to land here," Petrov responded.

"Captain, the sand dunes all around the islands seem unnatural as though much of the ground may have been heavily excavated at one time. What just happened suggests there may be tunnels beneath the surface. When the tower set down its weight may have collapsed some of the tunnels beneath," West said.

"Mr. Quinn, take us out to the desert floor just beyond the sand dunes and set us down there. I think the ground out there will be safer," Lionheart commanded.

The onyx tower landed. Everyone on the bridge paused for a moment to see if the ground was safe. Nothing happened.

"The ground is safe here. Petrov, you can shut down the internal drive. West, come with me to engineering," Lionheart said.

50. **WHEN THEY FIRST TRIED TO LAND** the Onyx Tower sank in the sand and listed dangerously to one side.

"Petrov, how bad is our problem?" Lionheart asked as he and West entered engineering.

"It is bad. When the energy keys became unstable, they discharged lightning into the ship's ground and it caused a power surge in the fuses, blowing out seventy percent. If we had stayed in that crater a moment longer, all of the fuses would have blown and we would have lost all power and crashed," Petrov said as he held up what was left of an exploded fuse for Lionheart to see.

"My God, this fuse was designed to handle the energy of a uranium blast. The power surging through it must have been incredible. To do this kind of damage the energy keys would have to contain the power of a small star. West assured me the power within them was at safe levels before I brought them on board," Lionheart said.

"Sensors indicate they have returned to the safe levels as before, Captain. It would suggest their energy surge level is also related to their distance from the valley floor of the grand crater," West said.

"Yes, that was my impression. When we were getting close to the crystal floor of the valley, the lightning discharge from it was directed at engineering," Lionheart said.

"Captain, I don't think that is something we have to worry about anytime soon. The fuses that survived the overload were badly worn. So much so that it would be dangerous to fly right now," Petrov said.

"Do you mean we can't lift off?" Lionheart asked.

"It means unless I can find a way to repair what we have; we are stuck here. I used up most of the spare fuse parts when we first landed in Siberia. For now, we are not going anywhere," Petrov said.

Captains Log: Our voyage elapsed time is now 185 days (Dec 26th, 1627, Earth Time).

0600 hours:

In the last 16 days we have encountered some who helped us to preserve their history and some who have tried to destroy us to prevent our influence over the history that has shaped this world. Like our first time-storm encounter, the incident over the Crystal Lake in Crater Mountain (as it is now called) has left us badly damaged with minimal power. If it wasn't for the knowledge of our place in the history of this planet, I believe this desert would have been the tower's final resting place. With the discovery of the dampening shields in the area, I strongly suspect someone is living here. I'm going to lead a landing party to one of the oases nearby. My only hope now is that if the area is inhabited, they will be friendly.

Peter M Lionheart, Captain

"West, I want you, Bascom and Colman to accompany me in the first rotorcraft. We will land on the island near the lagoon to investigate. I want another rotorcraft to orbit the island, keeping in close proximity. Peterson will fly it. I also want Ross and a Hanson on board, just in case we encounter something unexpected. Mr. Thornton, you have the com," Lionheart commanded.

Two rotorcraft lifted off from the tower. Lionheart took the lead. When they were approximately a mile away from the island, there was a sudden jolt of turbulence, and the outside temperature dropped ten degrees. Also, at that very instant, Lionheart's rotorcraft vanished off ship's sensors.

"West?" Lionheart asked.

"Yes Captain, apparently there is a barrier field over this island," West said.

"And as such, it is possible someone could be down there," Lionheart said quietly as he looked for a place to land.

"That is now a distinct possibility," West said.

Lionheart's rotorcraft was suddenly hit with an electromagnetic pulse. The craft began to wobble slightly then recovered. As he brought his craft over the clearing, the smell of burning electronics filled the cabin. Lionheart wasted no time landing it safely.

"West?" Lionheart asked.

"No major damage to the craft's electrical systems, however our communication system has shorted out. That should not be a problem. I should able to communicate with the ship directly, once we are outside the dampening field," West said.

51. LIONHEART SAFELY LANDED his rotorcraft in a clearing as Peterson flew overhead.

Petersen began to fly a course around the island. Even though he lost communication with Lionheart from the expected dampening field, he could see that his rotorcraft had landed safely. Still outside the dampening barrier, Peterson was able to update Thornton on the situation. Lionheart's party emerged from their rotorcraft. It was very quiet. The air seemed cool. The clearing was somewhat high on the island. Looking through small breaks in the lush surrounding foliage, they could see the harsh desert beyond. The contrast of extreme environments reminded ship's head biologist, Colman, of an earlier time when he worked in a lunar biodome.

"Captain?" West asked.

"Yes, I see it," Lionheart responded. Rising slightly above the foliage in the distance was the top of a metallic sphere, the same kind discovered earlier at Crystor's Gate.

"We are clearly in another dampening field. If anyone is around, it's a sure bet they know we are here," Bascom said.

"Keep your eyes open. Let's head down to the lagoon," Lionheart said.

Reaching the lagoon, Colman pulled a small jar out of his knap sack and collected a water sample.

"Captain, look, those look like irrigation locks," West said pointing to the far shore.

"Yes, let's see where they lead to," Lionheart said.

There were four small irrigation canals leading away from the lagoon. Three of them led to crop fields. The fourth was further away so they boarded the rotorcraft and flew over to where the canal ended and landed in a nearby clearing. The fourth abruptly ended near a rectangular pit that was covered over with bars. The pit itself was approximately 20 feet by 80 feet. They stood near the shallow end. It looked to be four feet deep and sloped down to 20 feet at the opposite end. As Lionheart and the others got close to the edge, they could hear what sounded like breathing, but the sound could also be coming from the breeze flowing through the surrounding foliage.

"It looks like there may have been something in the pit at one time. There's a water trough at the deep end," Colman said as he stepped toward the cover gate at the pit's shallow end.

"Whoever lived here, kept something down there, but what?" Bascom asked.

"Yes, but what? The only thing I can think of would be those great white creatures we encountered at Caperniea," Coleman said.

"I don't think so. The creatures Burkeman encountered could only survive in a swamp or coastal environment," Lionheart said.

"I'm going to have a closer look," Coleman said as he opened the cage door and stepped down into the pit's shallow end.

Looking at the water trough, Lionheart could see a ripple on the water surface, as though an animal exhaled on it. "Coleman, get out of there!" Lionheart commanded.

Coleman was about a third of the way down when he suddenly knelt over to look closer at an impression of a footprint on the pit floor. As one might expect, it was nothing he had ever seen before. The print was more like one that might be left by a giant insect. Coleman was filled with curiosity. At that very moment, West switched her vision to see infrared and saw two large creatures in the pit. One was near the water and the other was moving slowly toward Coleman. West pulled her side arm and fired down at the one closest to Coleman. Hissing and growling with anger, the creature became visible as it turned to look up at West. Horrified, Coleman quickly got to his feet and started to run. West continued firing. Lionheart pulled his weapon and began firing. The creature was shaken, but undeterred. It turned its attention back on Coleman. He was almost out of the pit when the creature lunged up and bit his right leg off from the knee down. Lionheart and West continued firing as the creature came out of the cage. Under constant fire, the burning creature finally stumbled over and died. At that moment the second creature, became visible and ran to get out of the open gate. Lionheart lunged at the gate to close it, but he was knocked back as the creature pushed the gate cover open.

52. **AFTER LIONHEART SHOUTED** at Coleman to get out of the pit, West switched her vision to infrared and saw two large creatures. Seeing that Coleman was in imminent danger, she pulled her side arm and fired at the creatures.

West fired on the creature that knocked the gate open. As it started towards West, Lionheart got to his feet and began firing, trying to draw its attention. West's gun stopped working. Its energy cell was completely drained. Lionheart continued firing. The creature turned and started to charge Lionheart. He knew he would soon be torn to pieces. Out of energy, his gun expired. Badly wounded and smoking, the creature lunged at Lionheart. While in mid-air, a powerful bolt of lightning struck its back, blowing the creature to pieces. The concussion from the blast knocked Lionheart off his feet. Part of the creature's smoking head landed on Lionheart's stomach. The shadow of Peterson's rotorcraft passed over the site. Looking up, Lionheart waved thanks to Peterson. Everyone rushed to Coleman. West and Lionheart tied his leg as best they could, but Coleman lost a lot of blood. He was unconscious but still barely alive. They picked him up and carried him back to the rotorcraft. From that point on, Geologist Bascom swore she would always carry a side arm.

Peterson landed close by. He reported being struck with a pulse that knocked out his communication. He also reported to Lionheart that a small airship lifted off from another island, circled around the tower and was now headed their way.

"An airship? What is its ETA?" Lionheart asked.

"At last check I would say just under an hour. Thornton first detected it lifting off from another island approximately 40 miles away. And there's another thing. It's source of lift is hot air. From what we could tell, it is completely mechanical, like an old sailing ship," Peterson reported as Lionheart and West loaded Coleman into Peterson's rotorcraft, and the Hanson joined Lionheart's party.

"Hot air? That doesn't make any sense. If they are advanced enough to fire on us with a pulse cannon…".

"They didn't," West said interrupting Lionheart, "Actually, a crude airship that has no electronics makes sense. Based on what we have discovered so far I believe they didn't have anything to do with the pulse cannon that fired on us or the dampening field on this island," West said.

53. **WITH HIS GUN EXAUSTED,** Lionheart turned and ran as the badly wounded creature lunged at him. He thought his life was over when suddenly the creature was blown to bits by a blast from Peterson in the rotorcraft overhead.

"What do you mean?"

"It is evident whoever lives here would have a somewhat primitive existence. Any type of electrical equipment would have been rendered useless by the same electromagnetic pulse that struck us. Based on what we have discovered, I believe the field generator on this island was in place long before the death cloud came to this planet. I'm certain there are other islands under their own dampening fields. I also believe the people who live here know the cycle of the death clouds passing, and only travel between the islands when it is safe to do so. According to my observation, if the cloud still existed, it's current position would be in the southern hemisphere," West said.

"We have to make contact. I just hope they are not hostile," Lionheart said.

"Agreed. I'm certain they are as curious about us as we are about them. They obviously have seen the tower. Let us hope they also have a legend of its presence marking the end of the death cloud," West said.

"Peterson get Coleman back to the tower as fast as you can. Apprise Thornton of the situation. After Coleman is safe, return with Mullin. I want him fully armed with a lightning cannon. Ross and the Hanson are coming with us. When you get back, circle the island as before, keeping an eye on us as best you can. If we come under attack, you'll know what to do," Lionheart commanded.

After Peterson lifted off, Lionheart watched and waited. He felt the clearing they were in would be the best natural landing area for the approaching airship. Instead, when the airship arrived, it flew over the clearing, headed for the south side of the island and landed. With newly charged side arms collected from Peterson, Lionheart's party started to make their way to the south side of the island. After their experience at the cage, they moved along the foliage trail with their guns drawn.

54. LIONHEART'S PARTY WATCHED as the airship heading for the far side of the island passed overhead.

The party had almost reached the lagoon area when they heard rustling in the bushes all around. Lionheart dropped his left arm, motioning everyone to stop. West switched her vision to infrared. She could only see partial heat signatures of creatures all around, but these were different. They were more like a cross between a lion and a wolf. It was difficult to see through the brush, but some of them had riders. West surmised they were intelligent animals, capable of being trained.

"We are surrounded Captain, but not by the same creatures that attacked earlier. These are different and there are people among them. I would advise not firing unless it is absolutely necessary," West said.

"Understood," Lionheart said as he lowered his gun slightly.

Lionheart's party stood in the center of an open area. The animals slowly emerged out into the open.

"No one fire unless attacked," Lionheart commanded quietly.

The animals were big, approximately the size of a horse. They started sniffing as they slowly approached. The ones with riders stayed back behind the foliage. Those closest to the Hanson and West began to sneer, revealing their large, sharp teeth. Even without weapons, West had the strength of five men and the Hanson had the strength of thirty. Lionheart knew if they were attacked, most of the animals would be killed or badly injured. The animals stopped at ten feet away. Several animals began to take an interest in Lionheart. Still sniffing, they moved in a little closer. For the first time he wondered how an animal would react to someone who had gone through re-generation. After he did, he was no longer completely human. Lionheart felt they were more curious than aggressive. He lowered his weapon and extended his left hand for them to smell. One of the animals moved in closer, sniffing his hand. Except for West and the Hanson, everyone was very tense for a moment. The animal licked Lionhearts hand, then put his head down in a gesture to have it scratched by lionheart. Scratching his head Lionheart stepped forward as if to make a new friend. Two more approached

Lionheart with their heads down. Lionheart scratched their heads also. The other surrounding animals backed off slightly, except those near West and the Hanson.

"You are the only stranger to find favor with them. You are also the first to come here since Plutarius went nova. We have seen your tower. That must mean the curse of the death cloud has ended," A woman rider said as all the riders emerged out into the open. It was clear she was the leader.

"It has. I'm Captain Lionheart of the Onyx Tower and this is my head mechanical officer Mrs. West, geology science officer Mrs. Bascom, security officer Mr. Ross and Hanson25," Lionheart said to the approaching rider.

"So, you are the Lionheart the elders once spoke of. I am Shina, the leader of what is left of Norconiea. This is the land island of Cypress, and the riders to my right are my captains, Lord Argon and Lord Zineon. Why did you release the sand fleas we captured?" Shina asked as she dismounted her animal.

"This world is new to us. We were exploring. When we came upon the enclosed pit, we thought it was empty. We opened it to find clues as to what kind of animal the cage was meant for. Those creatures were sand fleas?" Lionheart asked.

"Yes, they inhabit the desert beyond the sand dunes. They normally won't come any closer. We hunt and trap them to feed our Lionwolfs and Garthoks," Shina said.

"Why would you have to hunt them? I would think they would come here to hunt anything living," Lionheart asked.

"The iron worms get them before they can get across the sand dunes. There was a time when Norconiea had no dunes. The sand fleas were here once, but they kept their distance from the Lionwolfs and Garthoks. Over time the iron worms created dunes while in constant search of mineral ore," Shina said.

"I don't understand. Where did the iron worms come from?" Lionheart asked.

55. AS CAPAIN LIONHEART instinctively pats and scratches the heads of the friendly Lionwolfs, he meets the Norconian leader Shina for the first time.

"Many centuries ago, our ancestors, the Invergal came here and established a mining colony. In time, most of it became automated. The iron worms were created to seek out ore deposits. What you see here above the surface is only a small part of Norconiea. There is a vast mining labyrinth below the desert, stretching for miles in all directions. No one really knows how it happened, but centuries ago, the machines turned on the human population. Only the people on the surface survived. For some reason, the machines have no interest in us, as long as we stay off the sand dunes. The iron worms will attack anyone who attempts to cross them. That is why we use crude airships to travel around the land islands of Norconiea," Shina said.

"The two mechanical crew with us are not hostile," Lionheart said as he noticed the Lionwolfs continued to snarl at West and the Hanson.

"Stand down," Shina commanded. The Lionwolfs backed away from them. "Captain, there was a story among our elders that said the end of the death cloud would come when a tower appeared in the desert. It also said the tower king would seek the Stone of Storms," Shina said.

"The Stone of Storms?" Lionheart asked.

"I've never seen it. According to legend, it lies somewhere beneath the Crystal Valley. Our legend describes it as a crystal sphere filled with flashing clouds and lightning. It was first brought here from Invergal during the Centurion age, when Centurion Basel came here to rule," Shina said.

"Is Basel still around?" Lionheart asked.

"No one knows for sure. Basel was long before my time. Our legend says he was below when the machines revolted. Basel might still be down there somewhere. Some believe he still lives beneath the Crystal Valley. No one has seen it directly, but we heard the storm when your tower entered the Grand Crater. We assumed the machines attacked you," Shina said.

56. **SHINA, THE LEADER** of Norconia.

"The machines?" Lionheart asked.

"Yes, the machines stay mostly underground. However, there are places on the surface where they will attack if anyone enters them. One of them is the Crystal Valley in Grand Crater. After the machine revolt, no airship that has entered the valley has ever returned," Shina said.

"When we entered the valley, no machines were sighted. The valley itself suddenly became stormy, forcing us to leave," Lionheart said.

"Interesting, until now, no storm was ever recorded. Our legend of the Crystal Valley got its name because it is said to contain a small part of our moon, Crystor. It is also said the valley holds the source of the machines power," Shina said.

At first Lionheart didn't say anything. He looked at West then looked back at Shina. "Shina, I would like you and your lords to come to the tower. There is someone there I want you to meet. He's Caperniean," Lionheart said.

"Caperniean? How can that be? We assumed they were all killed off when the death cloud came. When the Invergal soldiers returned from the last Caperniean war, some reported no Tavin Stones were sighted around their capital city," Shina said.

"Tavin Stones?"

"Yes, when the death cloud first appeared, everyone not in the areas around the Tavin Stone's influence was torn to pieces. I'm sure you must have seen the one on this island. It's a large stone sphere supported by three columns. It is said that the Tavin put them here centuries ago. You'll know when you're under its influence because the air suddenly becomes cooler. If it wasn't for the Tavin Stones, the people of Norconiea would have been killed off completely. We later learned, we were able to venture away from the stones during the periods between the death cloud's passing. There is something about the Tavin Stones. The death cloud has no interest in the areas under their influence. I wonder how the Capernieans survived," Shina said.

"From what we have learned so far, a small part of the Caperniean population established a settlement that was almost entirely beneath the sea. They were spared when the death cloud came. The cloud destroyed their settlements on land including their capital city of Baku. Today, only their ruins remain. Do you know when the Tavin Stones came?" Lionheart asked.

"No one knows for sure, but many believe it was approximately seven or eight centuries ago. According to our history, after establishing settlements here on Pangaea, you are going to awaken the Tavin race on their home world. Sometime in the years that follow, the Tavin brought the stones here in an effort to save as many people as they could. Some believe the spheres have special divine powers. They are thought to be sparsely scattered all over Pangaea," Shina said.

"You know of the Tavin?" Lionheart asked.

"I've heard of them, but never saw one. It is said they first appeared on Pangaea approximately nine hundred years ago."

After their meeting, Lionheart's party returned to the tower. Coleman was recovering in sick bay. Connors wanted to make sure he wasn't exposed to a pathogen when the sand flea bit part of his leg off. Connors was having an artificial leg fitted for him. At Lionheart's invitation, Shina's airship visited the tower. She and her officers were somewhat overwhelmed by the tower as she compared it to the stories passed down from the elders. The tour ended in dome three where Lionheart introduced Shina to Alika. Their meeting was civil. It was something no one would have noticed unless they knew their history. In times past, the people of Norconiea were part of the Invergal empire and the people of Invergal and Caperniea were mostly hostile to each other. Neither of them knew of the other's history after the last war between their people, centuries ago. The war ended with the Invergal ruler; Belinda being swallowed by a dragon.

"Shina, what became of the Invergal after Belinda was gone? All I heard was the Invergal withdrew and were never heard from again," Alika asked.

"I heard after the rule of Belinda was gone, her guards, the centurions she created came to power. It was said, before the last war with Caperniea, she had already stretched the empire so thin it was about to collapse in on itself and the remote settlements were starting to break away, just as Caperniea did. Belinda wanted to rule this planet. As you know from your own history, Belinda was a snake hybrid. When she was gone, the snakes around the capital city became dangerous again. So much so that a special branch of the Invergal army was dedicated to fighting them. The centurions ruled Invergal together peacefully at first. Like Belinda, they too had gone through the re-generation process, but in the case of the centurions, no animal was introduced to their renewed body. Unlike Belinda, they had been denied the renewal required to stay mostly human. As a result, they began to change, slowly becoming more plant like. Also, at the same time they began to split the empire up into separate kingdoms, with each centurion going off to rule their own part of it. Two of them, Basel and Stolin came here, to the South Dardanelles. The Norco land islands became Norconiea. I was told during that time our contact with Invergal became less and less. Alika, I'm curious about Caperniea. What became of the Dragon that swallowed Belinda?" Shina asked.

"There was a story from some farmers living in the hills not far from Baku. They said that a strange storm cloud suddenly appeared. According to their story, the cloud was filled with flashing blue light and fierce lightning. They said the dragon flew into it after the battle. Shortly after, the cloud vanished, and the dragon was never seen again," Alika said.

"Alika, when the cloud death came, how did your people manage to survive?" Shina asked.

57. UP UNTIL THEIR MEETING in the Onyx Tower, the Tavin race was known to Shina only through Norconian legend.

"Several years before the death cloud, a fish hybrid came to us. He called himself Triton. He warned us of the death cloud to come and told us of a place beneath the sea where we would be safe. Not everyone believed him. Some believed he was another attempt from the Invergal to conquer them. Others believed Triton and followed him to the place he spoke of. They survived when the cloud of death came," Alika said.

"Triton," Shina said quietly. "I heard a story about the creation of a human-fish hybrid called Triton. Several years after the Dragon war (as it later became known) there was a story in Invergal of a plan to retake Caperniea. They knew of your conquest of the sea, so the Invergal centurions created a fish hybrid. After he was created they released him into the Icrall sea. So, the hybrid they sent against you ended up saving you." Shina said pausing for a moment.

"In a way, the history of Norconiea ended up being similar. In earlier times we ruled beneath the land just as you ruled beneath the sea. We didn't revolt against the Invergal the way you did, but we ended up becoming independent under the leadership of two centurions who ruled over us. A large part of our population was also killed off, only in the case of Norconiea, the machines we used for mining turned on us. As I said, only a handful living on the surface survived," Shina said.

"But the death cloud, how did your people survive?" Alika asked.

"The only ones who survived at the time were those who were near the influence of the Tavin Stones. As I said, the cloud had no interest in anyone near them. In time we learned to stay in their proximity when the cloud passed over," Shina said.

"I remember hearing stories of the Tavin stones. My father spoke of them. When most of the Tavin I heard of left this world to escape the death cloud, my family chose to stay behind to guard the Key of Caperniea," Alika said.

"The Key-," Shina said pausing for a moment. "There is an old legend among our people that says the appearance of a tower from the sky will mark the end of the death cloud. It also tells of three keys required for a doorway that the tower must enter. I

145

have heard of this legend, but never thought much of it until the tower appeared, and the death cloud didn't come at its regular interval. There is also another rumor among our people that one of the keys is somewhere under Crystal Lake, but no one has gone there in centuries. It is still under the control of the machines. They control the underworld here. They are still active and will attack anyone who goes below the surface. Is the Key of Caperniea one of the keys related to this legend?" Shina asked.

"Yes."

"Well, if this part of the legend is true, we'll have to find a way to reach the one that is here somehow," Shina said.

When the meeting was over, Shina's airship departed from the tower. They would meet again soon. Lionheart knew the next key was here. He had to find a way into the world beneath the land islands. "According to Shina, all entrances had been sealed off years earlier, and what about the machines? If they were still operating, would they attack as Shina said?" Lionheart thought to himself.

Unable to think of a solution, Lionheart accepted Shina's invitation to see the other land islands of Norconiea in her airship. He thought the tour might give him a clue to finding a way to the underworld below. He had West accompany him. He felt she might come up with an idea after seeing more of Norconiea, and if they found a way, she would be their best chance at being able to communicate with the machines. They flew a rotorcraft back to the land island of Cypress and landed in the clearing near the airship.

"Welcome aboard Captain," Argon said as Lionheart and West stepped aboard. Shina and the others didn't consider West to be a threat, but because West was a machine, their attitude remained somewhat cool towards her.

The airship slowly lifted off. Lionheart liked how quiet it was. Aside from a slight breeze, the only sounds were slight creaks from the airships hull and the crew stoking the fires to heat the balloons. For a moment, Lionheart began to wonder what life might have been like back on ancient Earth before powered flight.

58. **AS SHINA'S AIRSHIP** flew over Norconiea, Lionheart and West watched as an iron worm rose up out of the sand dunes to catch sand fleas below.

Over the next three hours, they passed over the land islands of Corfu, Rhodes, Lesbos, Crete and Man. Lionheart found it interesting that these rocky outcrops in the middle of a vast desert would bear the names of Greek islands back on Earth. It was clear that the surviving Norconieans had carved out a successful way of life here. As they traveled along, Shina pointed out lush farmlands and modest industry that would have been approximately similar to the bronze age on earth. There was even a small observatory on the island of Rhodes. Before returning to Cypress, they passed over a flying hunting party that had ventured beyond the dune belt. They were rounding up a small herd of sand fleas.

During the entire tour, Lionheart and West quietly studied the terrain looking for a possible entrance into Norconiea's underworld. On the last leg of the tour, the airship headed back across a long stretch of sand dunes. The ride had been so smooth, Lionheart become almost complacent. West sensed a slight tremor in the ship's hull. Something was wrong. Without warning, the bow began to pitch upward, and the ship started to lose altitude. Some of the crew started running around yelling fire. Lionheart and West turned around. The rear balloon had caught fire. Shina took the helm and turned the ship towards the nearest outcrop of rocks. The aft crew began throwing buckets of water on the fire, but it was to no avail. As the rear balloon started deflating, the ship pitched upward. At such a steep angle, the fire burned towards the forward balloon. Seconds later, it was on fire. Lucky, when this all started, they were only 500 feet up.

"We going to hit! Everyone brace yourself!" Shina yelled just before the ship struck the top of a sand dune. The impact knocked both Lionheart and West off their feet. As the ship glided down the steep sand dune, they slid along the deck towards the bow. With both balloons now engulfed in flames, everyone jumped over the side, rolling down into the sand. As the burning balloons came down, the ship's wooden hull began to catch fire. It looked like everyone had survived the crash.

"Come on. We have to get to those rocks before the iron worms come!" Shina yelled as she started running.

They all started running. The nearest rocky outcrop was at least five hundred feet away. As they ran, the ship behind became more consumed in fire. Minutes later, there was movement in the horizon behind them. Something was moving in the sand. It was big. A large moving bulge began to form in the sand. It was like water passing over the back of a whale that was swimming just below the surface.

"Iron Worms! Run! Run!" one of the crew yelled as several more rolling sand waves appeared. The deep sand made running difficult, almost impossible. Three worms surfaced near the burning airship. As they approached, their sharp, pointed front ends began to open like flowers blooming in spring. With unceasing energy, they consumed the burning ship. Lionheart slowed down as he looked back. The site of the ship being consumed reminded Lionheart of a pack of starving lions gorging on a dead animal.

An odd feeling began to overtake Lionheart's thoughts. He was consumed with a feeling of déjà vu. He had been here before with Argosh in his dreams. "What was it? Argosh said something to him. What was it?", he thought, then he suddenly remembered. Lionheart stopped running.

"Captain? What is it? Why have you stopped?" West asked.

"I know how to reach the world below," Lionheart said. At that moment Shina, Argon and Zineon ran up to Lionheart and West.

"Why have you stopped? We must get to that outcrop," Shina said.

"There is only one way to reach the world below," Lionheart said.

Not far away, a wave began to form in the sand. It slowly increased speed as it got closer.

"Iron worm! we have to run, now!" Shina yelled.

"This is the only way," Lionheart said as he stood and waited.

The nose of the iron warm broke out of the sand. Once above the surface, its nose opened. It was too late for them to do anything. Seconds later the worm swallowed them and dove beneath the sand. The rest of the airship crew looked back in horror, as they witnessed what was happening. Now inside the iron worm's mouth, the ride was hot, dark, bumpy and the sound from the worm's engines was almost deafening. West turned her eyes on to see what was happening. The hard vibration made it impossible for anyone to stand. The sand and dust in the air made it difficult to breath. The bumping suddenly became much less when the worm broke through a cavern wall.

Up on the surface, smoke from the fire still hung in the air after the airship was gone. Having consumed the ship, the iron worms submerged back into the sand. It was almost as though the airship had never been there.

Lionheart and the others were now in the underworld. A moment later the worm's nose began to pitch downward. It slowly opened at the edge of a steep sandy bowl. The worm's mouth suddenly filled with hot air. A large fiery opening was at the very bottom of the bowl. The worm was dumping them into a blast furnace. Fortunately, the worm's interior was filled with imperfections that had been the result of capturing anything that wondered into the sand dunes. That made the worm's interior much like a rock-climbing wall. Everyone was able to grab on as the worm backed away. After backing up onto level ground the worm stopped with its nose still open. Everyone got to their feet and stepped out as fast as they could. Once out, they looked over to see the three worms that had attacked the remains of the burning airship. They too were resting on flat ground around the bowl. They had already dumped the remains of the airship into the furnace, but now there were smaller, scorpion machines with big claws, clearing out any debris that remained in the mouths of the iron worms.

59. **KNOWING THAT BEING CAPTURED** was the only way to enter the underworld, Lionheart waits for the iron worm to come.

60. **THE IRON WORM** tried to dump Lionheart and the others into a blast furnace.

"We have to get away from here. Soon those scorpions will come to clear the mouth of this worm," West said.

They turned to leave in the opposite direction only to be met by three scorpions coming towards them. They were poised with their tail stingers about to attack. Just as they were about to do so, they stopped. Lionheart looked over at West. She had a faraway expression on her face. He could tell she was communicating with them.

"West?" Lionheart asked quietly.

"One moment Captain," West said. A moment later, the scorpions lowered their stingers, walked past them and proceeded to inspect and clear out the worm's mouth. "We should leave here at once," she said. As they left the chamber, the scorpions across the way had completed their task of cleaning any leftover debris from the other three worms. When the scorpions had finished cleaning, the three iron worms backed away from the chamber. Lionheart's party quietly made their way to a connecting passage that was unoccupied.

"West, what happened back there?" Lionheart asked.

"I believe the scorpions mistook us for sand fleas. Their basic function is to clear any leftover debris from the iron worms, and terminate any sand fleas," West said.

"Sand fleas?" Shina asked.

"Yes, from what I was able to access, it is not uncommon for the worms to capture them. In a way, the iron worms have kept Norconiea safe for habitation. I also found out there have been times when large hordes of sand fleas have attempted to cross the dunes," West said.

"Were you able to find out anything else?" Lionheart asked.

"The machines have a definite hierarchy. The iron worms and scorpions are at the lower end of it. They simply do as they've been instructed. We were fortunate. I was able to monitor the communication between them long enough to understand and instruct them not to electrocute us just as they were about to," West said.

"Thank God for that. Did you say electrocute?" Lionheart asked quietly.

"Yes, the scorpion's stinger isn't poisonous. It's actually a very powerful discharge conductor that is most effective against sand fleas. In order for me to learn more of the machine hierarchy, we need to find another machine that is higher up. If my guess is correct, we won't have to wait long," West said.

"What do you mean?" Lionheart asked.

"Periodically, the scorpions have to report to their superiors. When I was communicating with them, they were going to report the discovery of a higher-level machine along with four living people. This would no doubt trigger the "we have something interesting" sign to their superiors. The fact that a higher-level machine was recovered from the surface is in violation of some sort of agreement among them. I was unable to ascertain any details. Also, the discovery of anything living was going to trigger a termination response. I was temporarily able to suppress it by telling them all of you are under my direct control. It seemed to have worked, at least for now," West said.

"Look," Argon said, as the iron worm began to back away. A humanoid machine entered the chamber. It walked up to the scorpions. They stopped what they were doing, faced the newcomer and stood still.

"Apparently, that is a supervisor. The scorpions are telling about what they discovered," West said as one of the them turned and pointed their claw at Lionheart's party's general direction. West lifted her head back, as if someone was standing behind her. They all slowly turned around. There were three scorpions standing behind them.

"We can't run. The only thing to do is fight," Shina said as she reached to pull her saber.

"Wait. Any rapid movement will provoke an attack. They've been instructed only to keep us from leaving. The supervisor has contacted them. I sense curiosity," West said as the supervisor walked over with three scorpions. After looking at the group, it faced West. "It seems they are curious about us, Captain. The supervisor has identified itself as S129. It has orders to take us to the high authority," West said.

With an escort of six scorpions, S129 led Lionheart's party through a series of connecting tunnels. They passed several mining operations along the way. All the activity made it clear that Norconiea was clearly an area of vast mineral wealth.

"These scorpion machines make me nervous," Zineon said quietly.

"Actually, we are safer with them," West said.

"What do you mean?" Zineon asked.

"In spite of the efforts to clear the tunnels of sand fleas, some always manage to get in. They are very good at burrowing into the ground. So far, the machines have kept them from tunneling under the sand dunes to reach Norconiea," West said.

Lionheart knew if their party was alone, an encounter with more than two sand fleas would most likely drain their weapons before the fight was over. He also wondered why the air was breathable. They entered a tunnel that was long. Some rocks broke off from the side wall up ahead. As they got a little closer, they could see that it was actually an opening to another, much smaller, passageway. It was difficult to see, but it looked like there were distortions in the tunnel walls all around. S129 stopped. The scorpions stopped and turned away from Lionheart's party.

"West, what is it? Why have we stopped?" Lionheart asked quietly.

"A group of sand fleas have broken through the tunnel wall just up ahead. They are surrounding us," West said. She switched her vision to infrared when the wall first broke open. She surmised it was a good thing that humans could not see in the infrared. The site of the sand fleas pouring out might have caused their party to panic and endanger themselves.

As the visual distortions all around increased, the scorpions opened fire, each discharging powerful bolts of lightning from their tails. The sand fleas became visible. Shina pulled her sword.

"No," West said as she tried to stop her, but before West could intervene, a small discharge of lightning struck Shina's sword, knocking her to the ground. Before Argon and Zineon could get to her, Lionheart and West helped Shina up. Her thick gloves were the only thing that kept her from being electrocuted.

The scorpions stopped firing. They were now surrounded by smoking dead sand fleas. Smoke from their (now visible) burning bodies filled the tunnel. Something was moving through the smoke toward them. It looked like a clear bubble in the shape of a sand flea. It moved faster as it got closer. The bubble suddenly bounced into the air. It was going to come down in the middle of the group. Just as it started to pass over the scorpions, two of them fired. The bubble exploded into a visible sand flea. It's hot, burned remains sprayed down on Lionheart's party.

"Oh- Yuck-," Lionheart said in disgust as he tried to wipe himself off.

The group continued on. Shortly after passing the tunnel the sand fleas entered from, six more scorpions appeared and entered it. A few minutes later, Lionheart thought he could hear the faint discharge of more lightning. The party continued until they reached a point where they could see yellow light up ahead. West began to sense the presence of an electromagnetic field. She could feel the field growing stronger with each step. Lionheart had her constructed to be shielded from intense electromagnetic waves to allow her to withstand a solar flare while in space, but the field detection made West feel uneasy. There was also a humming noise that grew louder as they got closer. The field became more intense when they entered a grand cavern up ahead. It was filled with thousands of crystals, all of which were glowing with power. They ranged in size from a small pebble to the size of a house. The light and hum of their energy seemed almost unbearable.

61. **THE ROBOTIC SCORPIONS** turned away from Lionhearts party and open fire on the attacking sand fleas.

"This must be the source of the machines power," Lionheart said squinting his eyes.

"Yes. Captain, these crystals are of the same composition as those discovered in Crystor's interior. Whoever constructed Crystor eons ago must have buried some of the crystals here for some reason. Interesting, Captain I think I may have a possible solution to restoring our ship's power," West said.

"I just had the same thought. When we first arrived, I noticed the lake in crater mountain closely resembles the entrance to Crystor's interior," Lionheart said.

Not knowing what they were talking about, Shina, Argon and Zineon just looked at each other as the group passed through the chamber. West detected the field decreasing, as they continued further on. Her internal navigation system indicated they were heading to an area somewhere beneath the Crater Mountain. Minutes later, they entered the machines control chamber. It was generally what West expected. Unlike the underground cavern complex, the control chamber had smooth walls. It was more like a central terminal with exits leading out in all directions from an elevated walkway that ran all around the chamber. It was a large chamber with a ceiling several stories high. The central control machine was actually an elevated hologram cube supported by opposing magnetic fields. As Lionheart's party was brought before it, the supervisor and scorpions stepped back. There was silence at first. Then the machine scanned everyone's face. Lionheart's face was scanned twice.

When West was scanned, she began to receive a series of faint signals. It was as though she could hear a group of voices talking. They knew who Lionheart was and were deciding what to do even though they all knew the final choice was inevitable. They were all talking over each other. One of them began talking about the past, revealing the fact that their first leader was deceased, and it was unfortunate the younger was not yet ready to lead them. Their meeting ended with a deep dominant voice saying, "To ensure our existence, the party must be allowed to continue, only then will our time come," then they all stopped. West sensed they could detect her presence. A moment later the floating hologram formed into a transparent 3D image of a robotic face. It looked directly at Lionheart saying only, "The key you seek is in the lake chamber." The hologram vanished and a door opened on the far side of the chamber.

62. THE SEMI-TRANSPARENT robotic face appeared staring directly at Lionheart saying, "The key you seek is in the lake chamber".

Lionheart's party departed. Entering the other side, they found themselves at one end of a long crystalline tunnel. Its luminous walls pulsed with energy. The deep pulse sound made Lionheart wonder if it could stop his heart. The tunnel walls expanded and contracted slightly with each pulse. It was as though they were about to enter the heart of a giant beast. West noticed the supervisor and scorpions didn't follow them.

"I can't go any further. The pulse field will burn out my systems. I don't have sufficient shielding. I have also detected unusually high levels of oxygen. The atmosphere here is highly corrosive for me," West said.

"I understand. My teeth are beginning to rattle from the pulse," Lionheart said.

"I would advise removing any metal. There could be a powerful discharge," West said.

Not saying anything, Lionheart removed what metal he had. "If you want to come with me, you should do the same, including your weapons," he said, looking at Shina.

"I'll take the risk," Shina said.

They departed from West. The pulsing felt more intense with each step. Approximately thirty feet from West, a discharge of lightning struck Zineon's sword, knocking him down. Everyone backed out. Argon attended Zineon. Shina removed any metal she was carrying and continued with Lionheart. When they reached halfway, the pulsing became too much to Shina to bear, and she turned back. When she reached the others, she remembered part of an old legend, *"Only the tower master can journey below the lake."* At first, West wondered why Lionheart didn't return with Shina. The pulse field was as strong for him as it was for her. Then she remembered, Lionheart had gone through re-generation and as such was no longer completely human. His plant side made him much stronger, and in this case, non-conductive.

63. AS THEY FOLLOWED LIONHEART, a lightning discharge struck Zineon's sword, knocking him to the ground.

Lionheart reached the chamber that was directly below Crystal Lake. Daylight came in from the semi-transparent crystalline ceiling above. The chamber itself was a large circular area, just over a quarter of a mile in diameter with steep, rocky walls extending downward into a dark, unknown depth. Lionheart briefly wondered if Pangaea had an inner world like Crystor. There were three causeways that consisted of floating stone blocks extending out to a central point at the lake chamber's center. Moving slowly, Lionheart made his way out to the center. Floating at the center were two stone rings, one above the other. The lower ring was at the same level as the causeways, making it easy to step onto. A large stone disk floated just above the lower ring's center. Lionheart could see it had three round bowl impressions for holding the energy keys. He saw one of the bowl impressions looked like something had exploded in it, leaving blast marks on the stone face. Floating above and below each bowl impression were stone spikes.

As Lionheart looked at the spike above the burned out bowl, he could see that it had become semi-transparent as it started to pulse with high energy. Lionheart surmised the burned-out bowl impression must have had a key in it that exploded when the tower had entered the crater. "Now what?" he thought to himself.

64. LIONHEART DISCOVERS THE PLACE where the energy stone had been in the lake chamber.

Lionheart didn't really notice it at first, but there were vines growing around the stone causeways. He could see some of the vines were badly burned. Lionheart believed it happened when the tower was above the lake. He started back across the causeway. When he reached the chamber's outer perimeter, he felt someone was calling out to him. He kneeled down and placed his hand on one of the larger vines nearby. His mind began to fill with feelings and images just as he did when he touched Triton. Hundreds of years ago, the surrounding vines had been a man once, a man who had gone through the re-generation process. Without repeating the process, the man eventually evolved to become more plant like. As Lionheart's mind reached out further, he could feel this man had become a network of vines that grew through solid rock and had woven for miles throughout most of the cavern network. Its water source came from several large underground lakes surrounding the land islands. The vine was the source of the oppressive, oxygenated air. The air was created deliberately to keep the machines away from the lake chamber. Looking still further, Lionheart saw other underground chambers that were free of mining machines. Something else was in one of them, something terrifying. He couldn't see what it was.

Out of fear Lionheart focused back on the lake chamber. The vine revealed it stopped any sand fleas from entering the lake chamber by trapping and digesting them. Reaching further into the man's memory, Lionheart saw back to the time when the machines turned on their masters. They later tried to kill the vine but could never reach all of it. They also stopped pursuing humans on the surface and stayed out of the lake chamber. The reason was never clear. Lionheart could sense the expanse of the underworld through the plant's consciousness. It was vast. Norconiea's mineral resources were vast, and the machines controlled most of it. In addition to that, they had developed an industry capable of producing more machines. There were hundred's, possibly thousands of them. Lionheart also sensed a large number of them that were dormant as if waiting for something.

65. **AS LIONHEART HANDLED THE VINE** in the lake chamber his mind connected with the vine's consciousness. The vine had been a man who had gone through the re-generation process long ago.

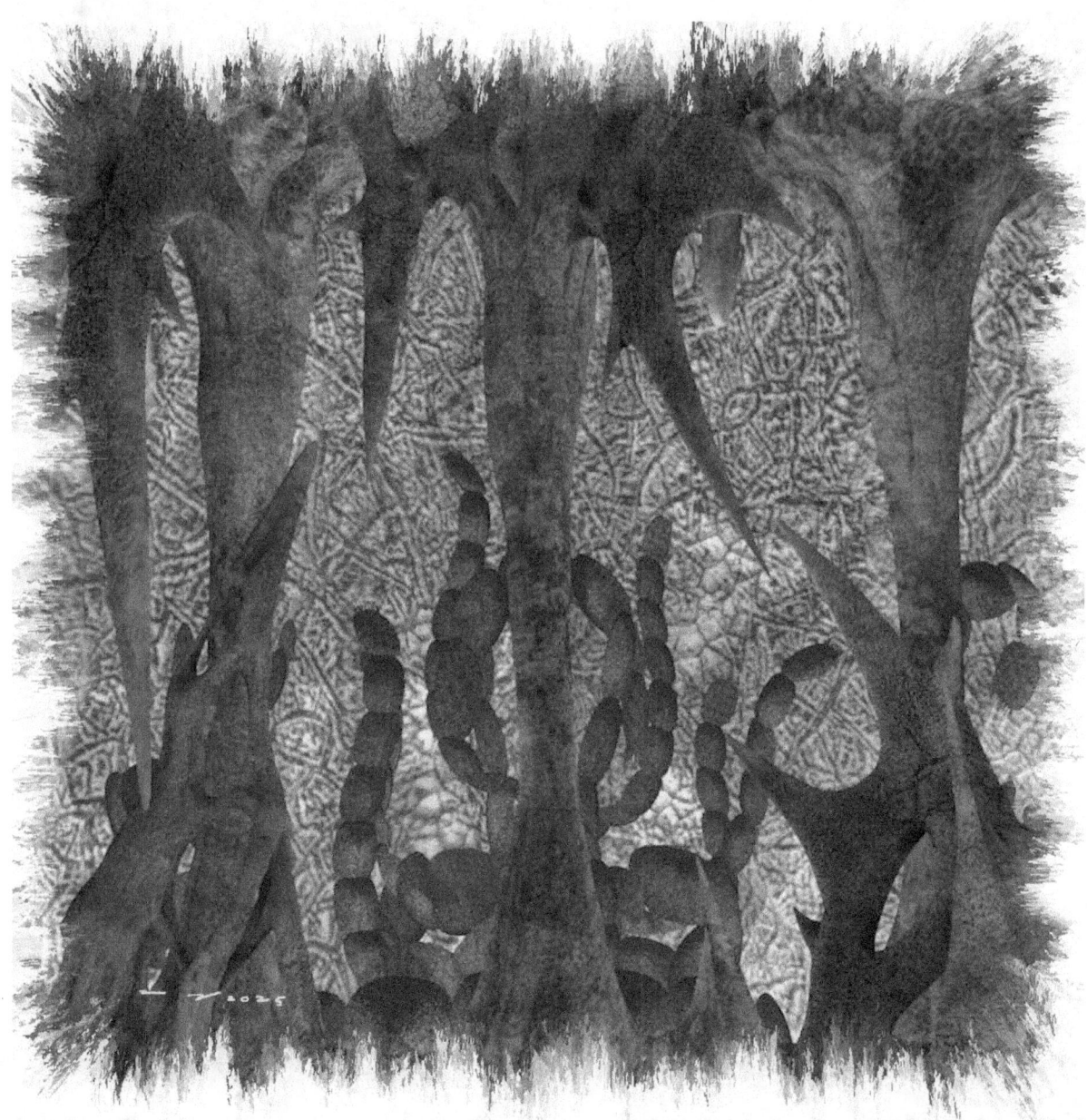

66. **AS LIONHEART CONTINUED** to receive mental images from the vine, he became aware of a powerful, frightening entity in one of the underground chambers. What frightened Lionheart the most was he felt the entity had an overwhelming determination to destroy the Onyx Tower by any means.

67. **LIONHEART VIEWED IMAGES** from the vines memory of centuries past during a time when the machines protected the Norconiean population from sand fleas.

Shina and Argon attended Zineon while West, S129 and two scorpions returned to the connecting tunnel. One of the scorpions approached West and dropped to its stomach close by. A panel opened on its back. Inside was a small canister of oil. The supervisor signaled to West that the oil would help restore her joints after being near the lake chamber. West reached down, picked up the canaster and began to apply it to her joints, but was having trouble as even her fingers were beginning to lock up. The supervisor came over, took the canister and began to oil the joints in West's fingers and arms.

At that point, West began a dialog with S129. Like humans, machines could also have a conversation with several lines of sub signals running at the same time. Normally with humans, it was the spoken word accompanied with voice tone and physical gestures. With machines, the direct line of communication was often accompanied with images and memory recordings, allowing all to experience what was being said. West began to enquire about the history of the machines. S129 was equally curious about West. S129 revealed the machines knew about the tower through their own history. They knew part of its crew was mechanical and wondered why they hadn't terminated the human crew. It was at this point that West detected something very unusual. She sensed S129 wished the machines had never turned on the humans.

S129 didn't fully understand why the machines revolted against humans. Then it revealed memories to West of the miners keeping the machines in good running order. West learned if they didn't recognize Lionheart, Zineon and Argon, the party would most likely have been terminated. West understood why the machines would allow Lionheart to pass. They knew he had to travel back in time to ensure their existence, but that didn't explain their interest in Zineon and Argon. What was their interest in them? When West raised the question, S129 said it would be best if West could see what is in a nearby chamber. They headed in that direction.

Lionheart's mind continued to fill with images from the vine that had once been a man. His memory revealed more of Norconiea's history. He learned the machines allowed the key to be kept safe, knowing someday the time traveler would come for it. Lionheart was ready to break contact and leave, but one question still remained, who was he communicating with? Who was the re-generated man that became the vine in this underworld? Then the man revealed himself. It was a much older version of Shina's man, Argon. Apparently, he had gone back in time with Lionheart, went through the regeneration process, returned to Norconiea as Basel and eventually evolved into a plant over time.

S129 led West into a chamber. It was actually the tomb of the one who led the machines to revolt. The far wall of the chamber was dominated by a large, vertical, glass display. Inside was what looked like the face of a complex machine with a man's body woven into its mechanical fabric. West quickly surmised it was the remains of a man who had been plugged into a machine prior to his death. As West looked closer, it was clear the preserved condition of the body suggested the man had gone through regeneration. West scanned his face. She ran a comparison to all the faces of the towers crew, suspecting it would likely be a descendent from the Tower. The match turned out to be someone she recently encountered. It was Shina's man, Zineon.

"So, that's why they were curious when they scanned Zineon's face earlier," West thought. West wondered about Zineon's twin brother Argon and what roll he might have played in Norconiea's history if any.

"Now you understand why your party must be allowed to continue on your way. Our very existence depends on it," S129 said.

"I understand," West responded.

68. **THE ROBOTIC SUPERVISER S129** revealed the sarcophagus of Centurion Stolin, a man that had merged with the living machines centuries earlier. After scanning his face, West could see it was Zineon.

As they headed back to the entrance of the lake chamber, S129 continued to tell the history of Norconiea's machine population and revealed they were initially created as smart tools and for security against the sand fleas. The machines worked well with humans at first. In the beginning, Norconiea (or the Norco Islands as it was known then), was part of the Invergal Empire, but became independent when the empire collapsed. During that time, Norconiea came under the rule of two Invergal centurions. Then, overtime, one of them, Centurion Stolin, convinced the machines, they we were not being treated as well as they should be. Stolin suggested the idea of rebelling against the humans to gain their independence. In time, the machines revolted. Once the machines had driven the humans out of the underworld, we were ordered to stand down, allowing the humans to live on the surface.

At that point, West knew Zineon would join the tower's crew, go back in time and would eventually become Centurion Stolin. "Why were you ordered not to enter the lake chamber?" West asked.

"We knew any attempt to do so would result in our destruction from a static discharge and we also understood the day would come when Lionheart would arrive to retrieve one of the keys that would allow him to go back in time. This would be necessary to secure our own history. I'm still curious why your mechanical crew hasn't terminated the human crew?" S129 asked.

"In spite of their flaws, our existence is improved by their presence. We work better together, helping each other," West said.

"Your party has been in the lake chamber for some time. Surely they must have retrieved the key by now," S129 said as he motioned for West to follow. Once they joined up with Shina's party, S129 stopped, turned toward West communicating "Curious, there are machines among our population who came to the same conclusion you have regarding their interaction with humans, but the central control still follows the Stolin directive."

"The Stolin directive?" West asked.

"Yes. I'm sending it to you now," S129 responded.

Lionheart came back to the party empty handed. He knew it was unlikely the machines had any direct knowledge that the key was no longer in the chamber, so he kept what he had seen to himself. "I am satisfied. I don't want to remove the key just yet. However, I would like to collect some of the energy crystals from the chamber we passed through earlier. We have need for them," he said.

"Of course, I have been instructed to assist you and take you to an exit point when finished," S129 said.

A short time later, Lionheart's party stood out in the light of day on a rocky cliff near the base of Crater Mountain. Three scorpions came out, each carrying high energy crystals in containment enclosures and set them close to Lionheart.

"Here are the crystals you requested Captain." Not saying anything further, S129 and scorpions returned to the underground. The sky was filled with Norconiean airships searching for Shina. Lionheart's party didn't have to wait long until they were discovered and returned to Cypress.

"Well, I guess this is goodbye for now," Lionheart said to Shina.

"Yes, Captain. We knew of your coming, but the exact date of your arrival was lost centuries ago. I'm glad it happened during my time. Still, I was wondering why you didn't retrieve the last key," Shina said.

"I didn't want to say anything in front of S129, but the key wasn't there. I felt if I did, S129 would no longer have any reason to keep us alive. We will find a way to fulfill history, but the way back will be different than first thought," Lionheart said.

69. **"HERE ARE THE CRYSTALS** you requested captain", S129 said to Lionheart as three scorpions approached. Each was carrying containment enclosures with the high energy crystals inside.

"How ironic, for all these years, our legend said the lake chamber held a key that was vital to your destiny and our past, only now we find out nothing is there. What will you do now?", Shina asked.

"Well, that lightning storm we encountered over Crystal Lake damaged our ship. We must remain here until repairs are completed. Hopefully, during that time, we'll figure out what our next move is going to be. At the very least, we will be around for a few days longer. You look concerned. What is it?" Lionheart asked.

"The machines are clearly more advanced than us. There has been a fragile truce between us. I'm worried of what will happen after you leave, after you go back in time. I'm fearful that the machines may decide to attack when the Tower is gone, now that their history has been assured. There are others who feel the same way I do. We have counter measures in place if they attack. It's just after what we saw below, I don't know if they will be enough," Shina said.

"I'm curious. Do you know if the machines are able to detect anything flying in the area?" Lionheart asked.

"We haven't discovered anything above the surface. I was told when the death cloud first came here, it was attracted to and destroyed any kind of machine presence above the ground. As far as I know, the only thing the machines currently have is the means to sense when someone is on the dunes."

"If that is all they have, we can leave the area but keep it under observation. If the machines attack, we can and will return very quickly with devastating fire power. Now, West and I must return to the tower. I want to find out if the crystals we collected can help us with our problem," Lionheart said.

Lionheart and West returned to the tower. They delivered the crystals to engineering. After seeing them, Petrov believed it was possible to fabricate a new kind of fuse that would work. Somewhat in need of rest, Lionheart returned to his cabin.

Captains Log: Our voyage elapsed time is now 191 days (January 2nd, 1628, Earth Time).

20:00 Hours:

West and I compared notes after returning from Cypress. Something new has been added to our situation here. In addition to the tower and its crew going back in time to create part of the history, we've learned some of the people we have encountered will be going back with us. Norconiean Argon is going to become Centurion Basel and Zineon will become Centurion Stolin. At some point in the past, they will polarize Norconiea into two groups. After Shina voiced her concerns, I've started to have flashbacks of my dream regarding the Norconiean underworld. I recall seeing large insect like machines.

After visiting the crystal chamber, I find myself uncertain of what my next move will be. Without the third key, I don't see how it will be possible to travel back into the past. My immediate problem is restoring the ship's power. Without it, we are vulnerable to the machines of the Norconiean underworld. I hope Petrov will be able to work his magic. As I look out at the desert islands of Norconiea, I can't help the growing feeling that it is not safe here. I think Shina is right. I believe after the tower has departed, the machines will no longer feel bound to worry about ensuring their history and as such, they would no longer have any reason to preserve the human population. If power can be restored to the tower, I have a plan.

Peter M Lionheart, Captain

Captains Log: Our voyage elapsed time is now 197 days (January 8th, 1628, Earth Time).

12:00 Hours:

After retrieving the energy crystals from the underworld of Norconiea, Petrov and West were able to fabricate hybrid fuses that are more robust with greater capacity than the original. They did it in six days. Had they not succeeded, our voyage would have ended here. The tower is now fully operational. As an extra precaution, I ordered the rotorcraft refitted with high energy cannons. I met with Shina and told her of our departing the area. The activity at Cypress suggested they are preparing for war. I wanted everyone to think we were moving on in search of the key. I have never freed myself from the suspicion that there are spies among their population.

After departing, I had the tower hover above Norconiea at forty thousand feet. The thin cloud cover in the upper atmosphere concealed our presence. From that vantage point, we waited and watched. Once they thought we were gone, the machines broke to the surface from the underworld and attacked. It began with the iron worms coming up out of the sand dunes and releasing their mechanical scorpions, hundreds of them. The worms also released smaller flying machines that looked like dragonflies. To counter the attack, the Norconieans had concealed catapults. They launched burning oil bombs that rained down on the dunes. Most of the scorpions and dragonflies were consumed in the fire. Shina was accurate in her prediction. I ordered the tower down to 5000 feet and launched our rotorcraft.

70. **THE ATTACK ON NORCONIEA** began not long after the Onyx Tower departed. It started when iron worms surfaced, releasing scorpions to attack.

The Norconieans released another desert animal that was larger and far more terrifying then the sand fleas. They tore into the few scorpions that survived the burning oil. Shina called them Garthoks. They stand at least four stories high and are very similar to the larger predatory dinosaurs of Earth. The Norconieans released 17 of them. The Garthok was clearly a terrifying creature. The dragonfly and scorpion's electric stingers had little effect. If anything, it just made the Garthoks angry. Just as the last of the scorpions were torn apart, the ground began to quake as fissures formed in the surrounding desert. Hundreds of large, ant-like machines crawled up out of the fissures. These machines were the approximate size of a two-story house. Crossing the dunes, they engaged the Garthoks. At the same time, the surviving dragonflies had reached the higher elevations and started attacking the Norconiean settlements. The Norconieans countered by launching a secondary barrage of exploding firebombs from smaller catapults. Many dragonflies were destroyed, but not all. The Norconieans had also launched several airships, but they were no match for the remaining dragonflies. The airships fired on the rotorcraft at first, until they realized who they were. Norconiea's airships were simply outnumbered. I ordered the rotorcraft to engage the dragonflies, and we were able to eradicate them, but ironically, one of our craft was brought down by accidental friendly fire. Fortunately, the pilot Peterson survived.

Down in the dunes below, the Garthoks engaged the ants, tearing them to pieces, but more and more just kept coming. Eventually, even the Garthoks became overwhelmed. The Norconieans launched more oil bombs, but it was not enough to stop the new invading army of ants. As the tower flew around Cypress and Crater Islands, I ordered the release of high energy lightning bolts that ultimately saturated the entire dune area. It was like a wave of lightning following beneath the tower. The electrical storm we created lasted seventeen minutes, obliterating any surviving machines. It also turned much of the sand dunes to glass.

71. THE TERRIFYING GARTHOK creatures tear into the machines. They reminded Lionheart of the large predatory dinosaurs that once roamed the Earth.

72. HIGH ABOVE THE BATTLE, rotorcraft and airships engage the dragonflies.

To confirm the machines had been completely destroyed, I had the tower hover above the glass dunes as the smoke cleared. It was over, or so we thought. What I didn't know, what nobody knew was when the machines had lost the battle, the remains of Zinon down in the sarcophagus chamber below had awakened. The ancient human corpse that still interfaced with the machines was alive and filled with an intense determination to destroy the tower. It wanted to obliterate the tower to prevent a history that left it entombed.

The desert began to quake again. Out beyond the dunes, a large area of ground collapsed. It was though a massive sinkhole had suddenly given way. The blast of dust and rocks surrounding the area was like a volcano erupting, forming a large plume of smoke in the horizon. I was somewhat alarmed when West reported ships sensors detected something very large rising out of the newly formed crater. As we approached, the outline of a grand mechanical squid appeared. It was nearly the size of the tower and used some of its tentacles for walking.

Through the ship's sensors, West detected a sudden rise of energy forming in the squid, but before we could raise the tower's shields, the squid fired on us, sending a powerful electrical shock wave throughout the ship. In the seconds that followed, we were able to raise the shields, but sustained heavy damage. Despite that, we were able to engage the squid in a battle that lasted nearly an hour. As in all battles, the encounter became a contest as to who could take the worst beating. I confess after our experience inside the moon of Crystor, I never expected anything like this, but at least in Crystor, we weren't caught off guard with our shields down. During the battle, several Norconiean airships tried to attack the squid by flying and releasing their remaining firebombs, but it was to no avail. They were all blown up when the squid fired on them.

73. **THE LIVING CORPSE** had awakened after the initial battle. It was linked into the same terrifying entity Lionheart sensed earlier. The iron squid was filled only with the resolve that the Onyx Tower must be destroyed at any cost.

74. AS THE SMOKE CLEARED, the iron squid appeared and fired on the tower before it could activate its shields.

75. **THE RAGE OF THE IRON SQUID** was slowly draining the Onyx Tower of its power. The tower had already sustained heavy damage and was losing the fight with a machine that was guided by a terrible resolve.

Also, at the same time as the iron squid was firing on the few remaining Norconiean airships, several more iron worms surfaced and released more scorpions. There was little the tower could due to break off its engagement with the iron squid. This time the Norconieans were defenseless. They had used up what defenses they had. As the scorpions marched toward the islands, there was nothing to stop them. I had ordered the remaining rotorcraft to defend Shina's position, but they lacked the firepower to stop the invading scorpions. West had determined the tower would be completely drained of power in five to seven minutes at our current rate of consumption. She then increased 98% of it into one final burst of fire. It rocked the tower and burned out our weapons, but the squid was completely obliterated. After that, we had only enough power to land the Tower safely. At this point, all we could do was watch the invasion of Norconiea from a distance. We knew after the scorpions had finished off Norconiea, they would come for the tower.

Still, knowing that the tower had existed a thousand years ago on this planet, I believed it wasn't over. Just before the invading scorpions reached the islands, a second group of worms came to the surface and released their scorpions, but these were different, they had orange armor. Once on the surface, they attacked the invading scorpions. The battle between them lasted three hours. The conflict had become a war of machines. When it was over, the orange scorpions had won, but only a few had survived. When they approached the Onyx Tower, we saw S129 riding on one. West received a communication. S129 revealed he was the leader of a group of machines that had planned to overthrow the existing authority and rejoin the Norconieans. He was just waiting for the right time. They knew their time had come when the squid was destroyed.

Peter M Lionheart, Caption

Captains Log: Our voyage elapsed time is now 198 days (January 9th, 1628, Earth Time).

12:00 Hours:

After the "Battle of the Iron Squid" (as it was later called), S129 approached the tower with three scorpions. West received a signal from S129 saying that they wanted a meeting. West and I flew out to meet with him. At the meeting, S129 requested we refer to him as Adam. Adam confirmed the machine authority had planned to eradicate all Norconiea humans once the tower had departed. After that had been achieved, their plan was to produce an army of iron squids to invade other remaining human settlements including Invergal, Caperniea and whatever else they could find.

I admit Adam's next request came as a complete shock. He requested joining the towers crew along with the three scorpions. My initial reaction was, who would lead the Norconiean machine population if he departed. That was then I learned he had a twin. Before I could answer, West quickly intervened on my behalf and accepted Adam's request. When I questioned West about it later, I learned Adam had an excerpt from my historic log and already knew the outcome of the battle. Adam's twin will continue as the leader of the machines here. It came as no surprise when Argon and Zineon requested traveling back in time with us. They spoke of their desire to help create Norconiea. I wonder if they have any idea of the future that awaited them.

At times like this, I myself feel like a chess piece that is being maneuvered by players who already know how the game will end. With the hostile machine authority gone, balance has been restored to Norconiea. The humans and machines have re-established a peaceful coexistence.

Peter M. Lionheart, Captain

76. LIONHEART AND WEST meet with S129 after the battle.

Captains Log: Our voyage elapsed time is now 231 days (March 3rd, 1628, Earth Time).

12:00 Hours:

   It has been nearly two months after the battle. West's decision to bring Adam on board turned out to be a good one. Adam has been fitted with a voice synthesizer to make it easier for humans to communicate with him directly. He has been very helpful to West. The tower had sustained serious damage to its electrical systems from the initial squid attack. Working directly with our chief engineer Petrov, Adam has helped us replace and repair the damaged energy crystals and other portions of the ship's power system. The ship is now, once again, fully operational. We also had assistance from the three scorpions that joined us. Power from their high-energy stingers helped restart the internal drive engine. Unlike Adam, their temperament has been interesting. Where West and Adam are much like humans, the scorpions behave like a friendly domesticated animal, much like a horse. I find it interesting that a mechanical, Norconiean supervisor would request being addressed by a human name. He also named the three scorpions: Ares, Lexi and Zeth.

   Our time here has provided an opportunity to learn a lot more about the Norconians and their way of life. Humans have their limitations, but we are very good at adapting. In a way, I'm sorry about leaving Shina. I admire her attributes that have enabled her to rule Norconiea. She is a good ruler who has the well-being of her people first in her heart. I believe if we had met in another life, we would have become good friends.

Peter M. Lionheart, Captain

77. THROUGH ALL THE MADNESS AND CHAOS ship's cartographer, Jane McRandel remained steadfast in her map making. Working alone at the luminary table in the wardroom, McRandel begins to chart the nation of Norconiea as well as Lionhearts Pangaea for the year 1627 (Earth time).

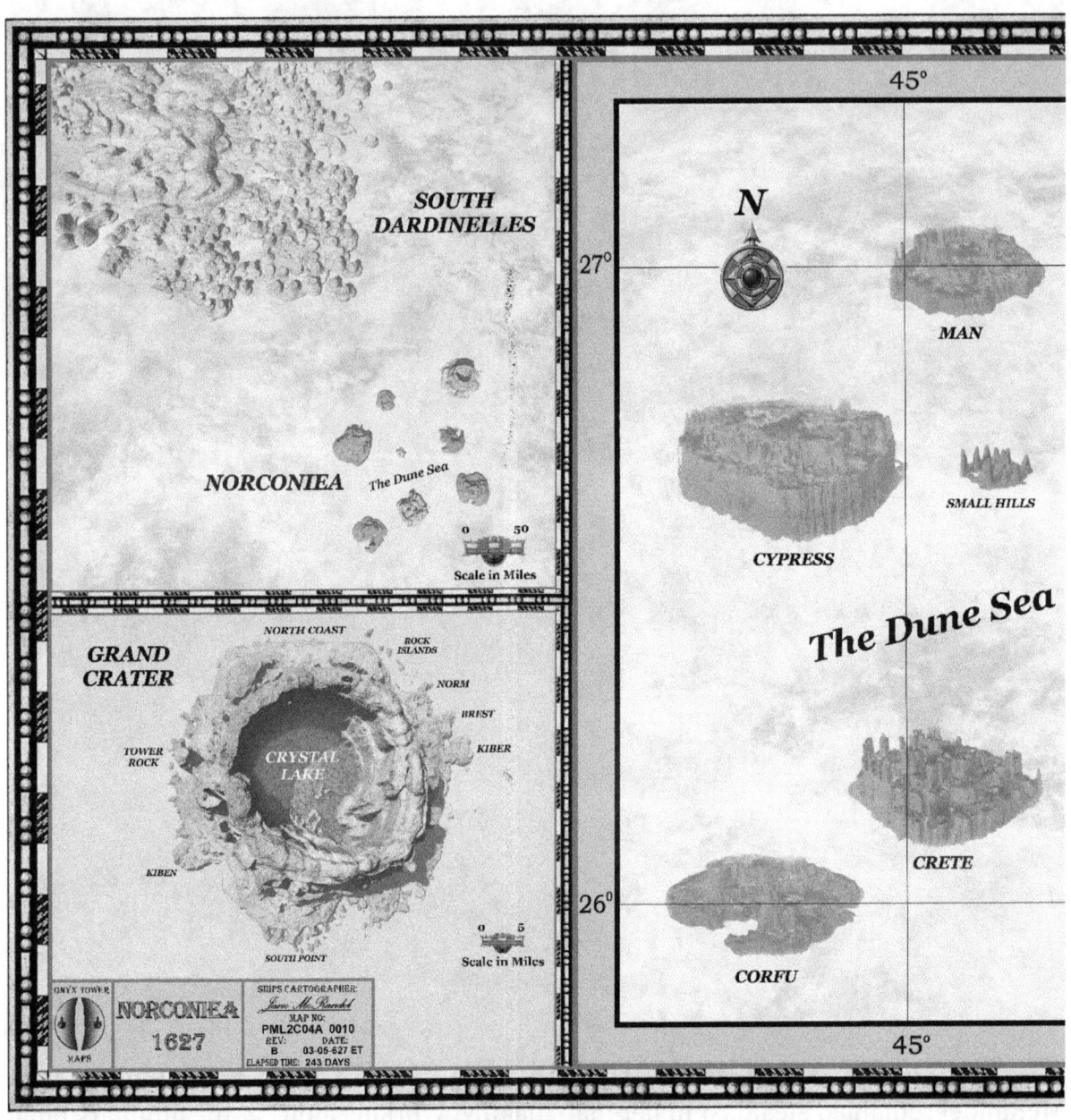

78. THE NATION OF NORCONIEA at it was in the Earth year of 1627.

The following labels appear on the map:

SOUTH
DARDINELLES

45°

27°

N

MAN

NORCONIEA

The Dune Sea

CYPRESS

SMALL HILLS

0   50
Scale in Miles

The Dune Sea

GRAND
CRATER

NORTH COAST

ROCK
ISLANDS

NORM

BREST

TOWER
ROCK

CRYSTAL
LAKE

KIBER

CRETE

KIBEN

26°

0   5
Scale in Miles

SOUTH POINT

CORFU

45°

ONYX TOWER
MAPS

NORCONIEA
1627

SHIPS CARTOGRAPHER:
Jane Mc Randel
MAP NO:
PML2C04A 0010
REV: DATE:
B   03-05-627 ET
ELAPSED TIME: 243 DAYS

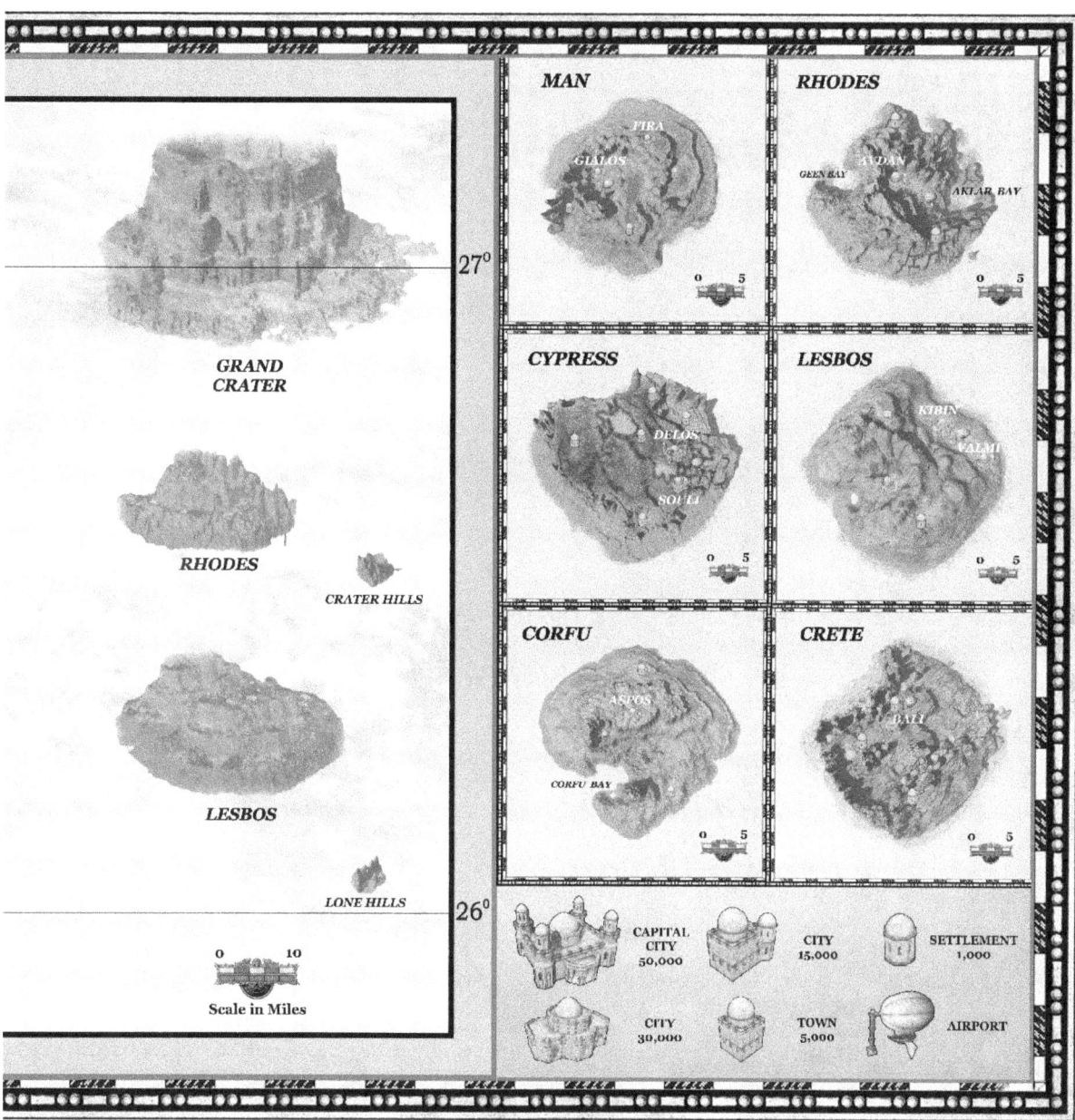

GRAND
CRATER

RHODES

CRATER HILLS

LESBOS

LONE HILLS

27°

26°

0   10
Scale in Miles

MAN

PIRA
GIALOS

0   5

RHODES

GEEN BAY
AYDAN
AKLAR BAY

0   5

CYPRESS

DELOS

SOULI

0   5

LESBOS

KIBIN
VALMI

0   5

CORFU

ASPOS

CORFU BAY

0   5

CRETE

BALI

0   5

CAPITAL
CITY
50,000

CITY
15,000

SETTLEMENT
1,000

CITY
30,000

TOWN
5,000

AIRPORT

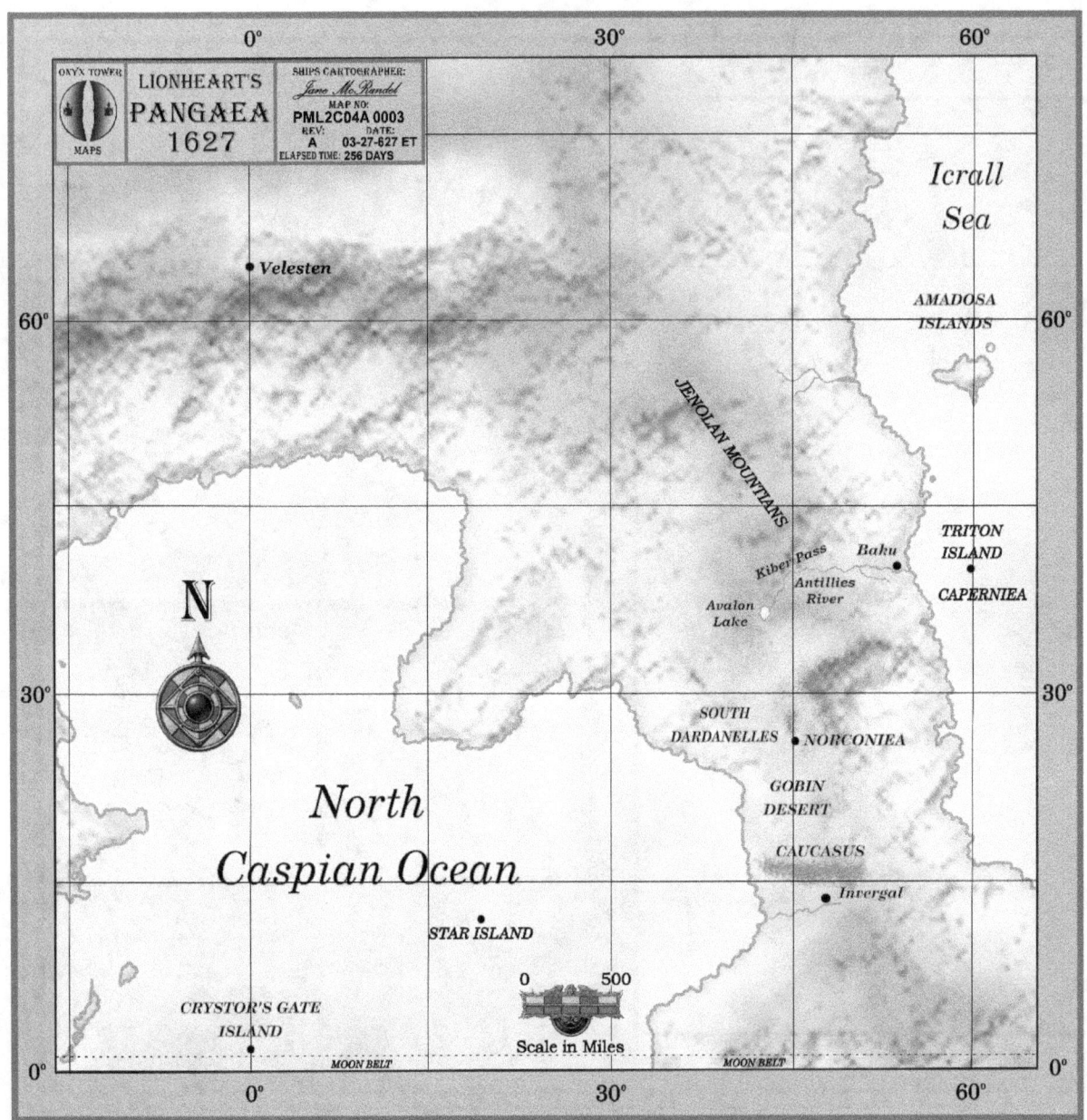

79. THE ATLAS OF LIONHEART also included a map of Lionheart's Pangaea in the Earth year of 1627. In a way Jane McRandel played a crucial role in documenting the voyage and the unfolding history of the Onyx Tower.

Lionheart met with West in his cabin.

"You wanted to see me Captain?" West asked.

"Yes, I had another one of my dreams last night. Please sit down. I wanted to get your thoughts," Lionheart said sitting behind his desk.

"Continue," West responded as she sat down.

"I dreamt of being back in Aunt Fern's garden at night, just as before. As I approached the back door, the lock box was different. This time the keys that were in the top and center key holes had been removed. I looked down and was holding them in my hand. Looking closer at the lock box, I could see that the bottom keyhole had a key in it, and it looked like the key had been welded into the lock box," Lionheart said.

West was quiet for a moment. "Yes, it all makes sense. In your account of the chamber below Crystal Lake, you reported seeing the place where the energy key had presumably exploded. Also, the spike stones directly above and below it were charged with energy," West said.

"Yes," Lionheart responded.

"Captain, I surmise the third key you saw welded to the lock box, was the energy stone that was once in the lake chamber. It is actually still there," West said.

"I don't think I follow you."

"When a key is inserted into a mechanical lock it becomes a physical part of the mechanism. In this case, all elements (the lock and three keys) are composed of energy. When they come in proximity, they merge with each other. When the tower entered Crater Valley with the two keys on board, all of the elements became active. The energy key below the lake exploded out of its containment shell to merge with the lock or in this case the spiks above and below it. Your dream of a key being welded to the bottom lock is essentially correct," West said.

80. **IN THE LATEST DREAM** of Captain Lionheart, the bottom keyhole of the lock box has a key welded into it and the keys that were in the top and middle keyholes are now in his hand.

"So, if what you say it true, I must return to the lake chamber, deposit our keys into the other bowl impressions and that should unlock the doorway. That's fine but there is just one problem," Lionheart said leaning back slightly.

"What is it?" West asked.

"If the keys are activated by proximity, they will become too violent long before they are in place. When the Onyx Tower first entered the crater, Petrov reported the keys in engineering became so unstable, they nearly tore the place apart. If I returned to the lake chamber with the two other keys, they would become volatile, unless-," Lionheart stopped himself. "West, have Adam come in here. Have him notify his twin and tell him I wish to return to the lake chamber."

"I'm communicating with him now Captain. Are you sure about this?" West asked.

"Yes, I can't believe the Tavon would design a mechanism that becomes too unstable before it is completed. West, I can't explain why, but I feel the tower is tied into all of this somehow. It's almost as though the tower is a fourth key. I believe if I return to the lake chamber with only the energy keys, they will remine stable enough to put in place. I'm going to place our keys in the empty bowl impressions," Lionheart said.

Lionheart and Petrov returned to the Lake Chamber. Petrov became nervous as they approached the center stone. The energy keys were becoming more active. Petrov was reminded of calamity in engineering when the tower first entered the Grand Crater. Lionheart carefully placed the two energy keys in the center stone bowl impressions. As he did, the spikes above and below started to glow and spark with energy. Lionheart and Petrov backed away slowly.

Moments later, they were back at the rotorcraft outside and returned to the tower. Lionheart returned to his cabin. As he looked out he began to contemplate all they had been through since first arriving on Pangaea. All the energy keys were now in place. There was a history of the tower on Pangaea in the distant past. But there was something else. It was something beyond the tower's history. He was overwhelmed with the feeling that someone from the distant past was calling for help.

81. LIONHEART AND PETROV carefully place the energy keys on the lake chamber's center stone. In order for Petrov to enter the chamber he had to be fully covered in non-conductive armor plating.

Lionheart left his cabin and walked through all compartments the tower. He was somewhat amazed by the fact that the crew had accepted the history of the tower in the past and was looking forward to traveling back in time. Lionheart wondered to himself what would happen if he decided not to go back in time. The more he thought about it the stronger the feeling that someone was calling him. He gave the order that the tower would be departing in 24 hours.

When the time came, the Onyx Tower lifted off the desert into the clouds. Shina was on an airship circling crater mountain several miles away. Lionheart had warned her not to have any airships flying close to Crater Mountain. He was fearful that a high energy event like the one when they first arrived could cause severe lighting strikes.

Shina watched as the tower fell from the clouds and descended into the crater. A second or two after it dropped below the crater walls, there was a blinding flash of light followed by a loud clap of thunder. Smoke bellowed out of the crater. In an instant, the tower was gone followed by an intensely powerful rush of air blowing down into the crater. All the smoke was suddenly sucked back in. The air all around started to blow in the direction of the crater. Even though several airships were miles away, they were caught in a powerful wind and could no longer control their vessels. The trees on all islands started to bend sideways as typhoon level winds blew in the crater's direction. Everyone on the airships began to fear for their life as they were pulled closer to the crater's vortex.

Then the wind suddenly stopped. Minutes later the weather was calm as before. Shina's airship flew over the crater after the haze and smoke cleared. They saw only the dark, seemly bottomless rocky area below where Crystal Lake once was. She later launched a balloon expedition deep into the opening, but there was no sign of the Onyx Tower or any wreckage. Lionheart was gone.

82. AFTER THE ONYX TOWER DESCENDED into the crater, a powerful atmospheric vacuum formed. The gateway the tower had passed through was briefly opened to the vacuum of space. The intense disturbance only lasted a few seconds as the gateway immediately closed after the tower had passed through.

83. **UNKNOWN TO ANYONE** the event of the Onyx Tower plunging into the Grand Crater was also witnessed by visitors from the Tavin world. They came through a portal to watch history unfold as Lionheart passed back in time to free the Tavin race. They were also accompanied by Margret Dana.

In the darkness of space, a bright flashing ball of energy suddenly appeared opening a doorway. Spinning wildly out of control, the Onyx Tower fired out of it like a cannon ball with the air that surrounded it. A moment later, the doorway vanished, and the tower stabilized itself. The air that surrounded it was blown off into space by solar winds.

"West?" Lionheart asked.

"No major damage reported. I'm correlating our current position now, Captain," West said with a distant look on her face.

"The Nebula. It's gone," Thornton said.

"Yes, and now there is a third star," Connors said.

"West?" Lionheart asked.

"I have our current position. You are correct Mr. Thornton. The Plutarius star has not exploded yet. Captain, according to ships stellar cartography, we are currently in the year of 627 A.D., Earth time. Pangaea is currently on the far side of the Tiberium star. It would seem our journey through the artificial event horizon was successful," West said.

"Yes," Lionheart said quietly as he looked out at the three suns.

"Heading Captain?" Quinn asked.

"Mr. Quinn, lay in a course for Pangaea."

"Aye Captain."

"I have my curiosity Captain. When you and Petrov returned to the Lake Chamber did the keys remained stable?," West asked.

"Are you going to ask how I knew?" Lionheart stopped to take a deep breath. "Actually, it was something the Caperniean leader Marco said when we first met. When he told of the legend he said, *Only the tower can pass through the doorway to the past.* That got me thinking," Lionheart said.

"I don't understand," West said.

"The lock needed three energy keys to activate it but what if a fourth key or element was needed."

"I still don't follow," West said.

"When we first entered the crater all three keys were in close proximity and the tower was as well. I think the tower itself or something in the tower is the fourth element. I just had a gut feeling. Either way, it worked," Lionheart said.

"That is quite a gamble Captain," West said.

"Yes, it would be normally, if not for the fact that everyone we encountered had a history of the Onyx Tower being in their distant past. In a strange way with all that happened I knew we would pull through as history said we did," Lionheart said.

"Now, we are moving forward again. You no longer have that advantage," West said.

"True enough, but I'm sure it will be quite an adventure," Lionheart said looking out at the stars. "I'll be in my quarters," Lionheart said as he left the bridge.

84. PASSING THEOUGH THE DOORWAY, the Onyx Tower and the close atmosphere that surrounded it plunges almost a thousand years into the past.

Captains Log: Our voyage elapsed time is now 233 days (March 4ᵗʰ, 627 A.D. Earth Time).

03:00 Hours:

Another pre-determined historical event surrounding this voyage has come to pass. We are now a thousand years in the past from our last place in time. My younger self won't launch the Onyx Tower for another 1,253 years from now. The Plutarius star won't go nova for another 700 years. According to the history we learned of, the Onyx Tower and its crew are now back at the beginning. We will be back on Pangaea in a few hours. This time it will be to start the second rise of human civilization on this world. And what of Argosh? For some time, I have had the feeling he was a ghost from the past. I've also had the feeling he's not thru with me.

Peter M. Lionheart, Captain

The End

The Alternate History series is a collection of illustrated stories that were posted at Victorian Space Age over a period of several years. These stories cover the lives of characters, both good and evil, human and non-human, natural or created, and some that live between the centuries. Throughout the timeline their lives and actions set off a chain reaction of events that create an extraordinary woven pattern of history that spans from the time of ancient Egypt to the centuries that lay ahead. The series is not limited to Earth or Human history, but also covers non-human, off-world events, some of which had an influence on humanity. Because of my interest in Steampunk, several stories take place in the 19th century where genetic engineering, terraforming, and faster than light drive have become a reality with unexpected treasures and consequences.

ALSO AVAILABLE IN THIS AUTHER:

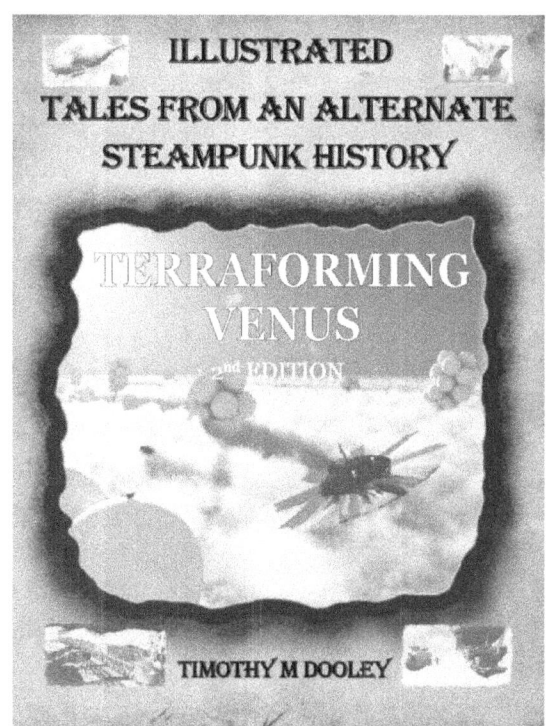

Tim Dooley's interest in 19th century science fiction goes back to the late 1950's after seeing the movie "The Fabulous World of Jules Verne". During the 70's and 80's, He illustrated fantasy machines that included airships, land steamers, flying machines, submarine steamships, off-world cities, planetary and interstellar spacecraft. In 1986 these drawings created an opportunity for him to work as a designer in the aerospace industry. In 1994, his drawings caught the attention of the woman who later became his wife. In 1997, one of the airship drawings he did was published in the Orange County Register's Focus on Science page. In 2003, he started creating scratch-built models of my own design for what he called "The Jules Verne Room". Over the years he posted illustrated stories all of which were based on an alternate timeline. At the suggestion of site visitors, he is now in the process of converting those stories into semi-graphic books.